I0672572

Prowler

A Global Paranormal Security Agency Story

Jodi Kendrick

SoulGate Publishing

Dragon Island
Dragon Heat

Enchanted Ardor
Wish

EveL Worlds : FUCN'A
Tough Nut
Diamond in the Ruff
Honeyed Nut
Gorilla in the Hiss
FUCN'A Collection One
Pedigree Collection

Finely Aged
Dragon Steel

Global Paranormal Security Agency
Awakened
Surfacing
Polestar
Aquatic Investigations
Prowler

The Kindred Chronicles
Healer
Mercenary

The Soaring Dragon Chronicles
Return Flight
Changeling

The Global Paranormal Security Agency

The Global Paranormal Security Agency is a hidden investigative group dedicated to bridging the paranormal and human worlds to keep everyone safe.

Protect. Defend. Seek Justice.

Thank you!
To my family, friends and writing community.
Your continued love, support and encourage-
ment keep me going.
Without you, I'd still be dabbling and drifting.

Jess, thanks for *ALL* the things in this whirlwind
you've instigated!

Kim, thank you for all the work you do to make
my words make sense!

My deep appreciation goes out to **Milly Taiden**
for her generosity in opening her creative
worlds to those of us that enjoy playing in
them!

For My TeddyBear'

ONE

PIA JENSEN GRUNTED AS she thumbed past another text and tossed her phone on the passenger seat beside her.

Erin had just bailed on her, again.

Pia's squad lead, Tamara Cole, at the Global Paranormal Security Agency had encouraged her to integrate further with the Montreal police department she was embedded with, but she was only here for a couple more months, then she would be reassigned.

Mingle. Socialize. People.

The last year had been hard, and 'peopling' was very low on her list of priorities.

She missed her team. A team of kick-ass women GPSA agents. It was the one place where she'd finally felt like she belonged. And here, in Montreal, she was alone and still working solo. *Mostly* alone.

Her old friend and sometimes lover, Erin lived here but...she was busy with the chaos of running her club.

Pia sighed, swallowed some coffee from her favorite travel mug to lessen the sting, and acknowledged that this placement had been at her request.

For her dad.

She gulped more coffee, this time to bury the sharp rise of grief.

Her sensitive hearing picked up the growl of an expensive engine, gearing up. The speed radar triggered as a black sports car blew past her concealed location.

Time to go.

With a cursory glance for oncoming traffic, she threw the cruiser into drive, hit the gas, siren, and lights, speeding off in pursuit.

First thing in the morning, too.

These assholes in their tailored cars seemed to think speed limits were vague suggestions—simply inapplicable to them.

Probably another weaselly twenty-seven-year-old living off Mummy and Daddy's millions.

Following the car as it rolled to a stop on the hard shoulder, she killed the siren, then called in the license plate. She left the cruiser lights in their loop as she exited the car.

Pia sighed, putting her bitch face on, mentally prepared for some bullshit as she strode alongside the F-Type Jaguar, resisting the urge to trail a finger along its sleek fender.

The window eased down and a darkly tanned hand with long fingers extended identification details. The arm was encased in a crisp gray suit sleeve with working buttons. The cuff obscured the edges of black ink on the man's skin. An Aikon glinted in the sunlight. Bergamot and black pepper tickled her sensitive nose as his aftershave, mingled with the undertone of his personal scent, drifted toward her on the morning breeze.

Human.

Her inner kitty's attention was piqued.

"Good morning, sir." Fingertips resting on her hips, she took the last step up to the window, ignoring the proffered identification. "Are you aware we have speed limits in this city?"

"Yes. I'm late for work." Shadows obscured the driver's profile, with his face turned away as he scrolled through messages on his phone.

She didn't miss the Spanish accent.

Pia's teeth ground. Arrogant prick wasn't even deigning to pay attention to her.

"Late for work or not, you were driving thirty kilometers over the limit for this zone. There are kids and seniors that have places to go, too," she said, doubting her point would have any affect.

He put his phone down and turned to look up at her.

Had she stopped breathing? Damn... *Damn*! She knew that face. It adorned a thirty-foot banner next to the front doors outside the local soccer stadium.

Renni 'The Pitch Prowler' Diaz.

Her stomach quivered.

The tickets in her locker at the station were for the derby that night. Both of Montreal's professional soccer teams would be going head-to-head. He was expected to appear on the starting lineup. The growing rivalry between the teams promised excitement on the field. She'd been looking forward to this game, all week.

And he was so *damned* hot.

She steeled herself against the fan girl excitement gathering in her stomach, threatening to erupt in a juvenile giggle.

Her eyes drank in the view for a moment. That mouth. She'd fantasized about those lips, many nights.

"Yeah, listen, I really am in a hurry after a meeting that ran late this morning. Can we just call it a warning and I'll be on my way? I promise to be mindful in the future," he said, tossing her a grin.

Pia straightened. "I see." Disappointment steamrolled her as she pulled her pen and pad from its place on her vest, taking her time. Plucking the cards from his still-extended hand, she began to fill out the speeding ticket.

"Do you like sports?" He turned his wrist, glancing at his watch. "I can get you tickets to tonight's soccer match. Bring a friend?"

Her eyes flicked up from her pad, just having written his name. Renni Diaz. His address told her he'd been coming from home, heading for the training facility. After being embedded with local law enforcement for the last year, she was getting to know the city districts well enough.

"Already going," she grunted.

"Ah wonderful. Perhaps we'll see each other later tonight." He let his gaze sweep her from head to hip, before resting on her face, brow quirking.

Was he seriously trying to flirt his way out of a ticket?

It wasn't like he couldn't afford to pay it...

Image.

Speeding tickets didn't look good on a high-profile personality's image.

She shrugged. Not her problem.

She finished writing up the ticket, handing it to him. "Good luck tonight." She turned, stepping toward her cruiser.

His fingers ghosted hers as he accepted the slip of paper. "Will I see you after the game..." He glanced at the ticket. "Constable Jensen?"

Glancing back, she quirked a brow, ignoring the shiver caused by his touch. "I will be joining some friends for drinks downtown."

If Erin didn't bail on that too.

He squinted at her, considering. "L'Auberge, Dominion or Chatton Noir?"

That was a pretty specific short list. "Chatton Noir," she said, surprised.

"I have friends on the force, too." He grinned again.

"Have a good day." She dismissed him, again turning toward her cruiser.

"I'll see you tonight," he said as he pulled away from the curb, resuming his drive. At the stop sign, he gunned the engine a couple of times, pulling her attention to see if he was going to speed away.

He didn't.

Instead, he waved and turned the corner.

Weird.

She dropped back into the driver's seat of her cruiser with a snort.

She couldn't help pondering the image he'd conjured of meeting her at the bar later.

Bullshit.

Too bad; it dulled the shine of her fantasy of him a little.

Except for how hot he was. So much better in person. And he smelled amazing.

A guy like that wasn't going to just show up at a pub looking for her.

With a grunt, she dismissed that train of thought and put her cruiser into gear.

Back to work.

TWO

THE SPEEDING TICKET BURNED a hole in Renni's pocket as he parked his Jag. He jogged into the training facility where the team meeting was being held before the day's game. He really hadn't meant to be late again; he'd just gotten caught up on his way out the door.

Constable Jensen. Damn, they had good looking cops in this city. Why hadn't he come here sooner? He smiled to himself as his mind was already lost in those incredible cat-like golden eyes.

He turned the corner and pushed the door open to the meeting auditorium, his smile faltering. Management was already onto phase two of the tactical meeting.

Everyone from management—and personal assistants, including training and equipment staff—was present.

"Glad you could find the time to join us, Diaz," Club Manager Daniel Smith said, expression tight, as he glared at Renni.

Renni nodded and slid onto a nearby seat.

"Kids again?" His teammate, Ben Wong, whispered from a row over.

Renni grinned, sliding his right fist across his chest, flashing the bright pink pony stamp on the back of his hand.

Ben laughed, shaking his head.

Smith stopped talking. "Care to share?" He tapped the dry-erase marker on the board then capped it, turning to Renni.

Renni sighed, spreading his hands. "Just showing off the fancy new ink I got from my neighbor this morning as payment for teaching her how to dribble."

In front of him, Omar Naas turned to look. "My kid has that same stamp." He grinned at Renni.

Smith cut in. "We have a game to focus on."

Renni shrugged. "Fans come first, right, boss?"

Smith scowled at him, saying nothing more on the matter as he turned back to his presentation.

They had a lot of material to cover. Tonight's derby was a big deal.

Renni had been late again. He doubted Smith was going to let it slide. He'd be lucky if Smith didn't bench him.

He sighed, focusing.

Renni's brain was ten pounds heavier after the meeting as they all got up to head for the facility's dining lounge for the ritual pre-game meal. Throughout the afternoon, he chatted with teammates and colleagues. Everyone was at ease, drifting from jokes and stories about their families to the upcoming game and back again.

He enjoyed the ebb and flow of team life. *His* life. Renni hadn't been in Montreal long—just about a year now. He was finally starting to settle in. Except where the manager was concerned.

Taking the last few bites of his meal, he looked up to see Rosa Russo, the shoe manager, signaling him to come and see her later. He gave her a thumbs up. She smiled that contagious smile of hers, then spun her wheelchair and disappeared down the hall.

"What's funny?" Ben Wong asked, sliding onto the chair beside Renni.

"Huh?"

"You've got a goofy grin on your face."

Renni laughed. "Nothing, just Rosa."

"I like her," Ben said, "Always so friendly and happy. She's good for the environment."

"Reminds me of a cousin back in Argentina." He paused a moment, thinking of his childhood home. "It's winter there now. Nothing like winter here, though." He laughed.

"You were here over winter?" Ben shuddered. He was a new transfer, having arrived several weeks before.

Renni nodded.

Ben raised a brow. "And you're still here."

Renni shrugged. "I like it here. So far, anyway."

"Maybe there's still hope for me." Ben clapped Renni on the back as he rose from his chair. "Got any winter survival tips?"

Renni shrugged as he, too, rose from the table, picking up his plate to leave it at the dish station. "Warm your bed with a beautiful woman."

"That's a given." Ben's brows rose. "What else you got?"

"That's all you need. I'm heading to a pub after the game, want to come along?" Renni said rising to his feet.

Ben tilted his head back and forth considering, then shrugged as he fell instep beside Renni. "Thinking we can get into as much trouble as we did in Barcelona?"

Renni laughed at the reference to their early days as young footballers prowling the club scene across Europe when they met for friendly matches.

"Anyway, maybe next time; I've already got a date with a beautiful local that's going to teach me Montreal French." Ben said.

"Preparing for winter?" Renni grinned.

"Maybe," Ben said, returning the grin as he wandered away.

Renni continued on toward Rosa's domain. Voices drifted toward him as he made his way down the hall. He recognized the voices as he stepped into the open doorway, unnoticed. Sophy Khienak's back was to him as she spoke to Rosa over the shoe room's main counter, her stance was more an intimidating pose than casual chat.

"...it doesn't matter, I'm negotiating a big contract with the company, so we'll be replacing all of their shoes."

"I told you, we don't have the rights to do that. It's asking for trouble to just switch out their footwear—it's a vital part of their equipment and highly personalized." Rosa crossed her arms, leaning away from Sophy's encroachment, despite the counter between them. Rosa's tone was clearly exacerbated.

"I don't care. Just be ready when the shipment comes in." Sophy said, tossing a long blond curl over her shoulder.

Rosa's eyes flicked to Renni in the doorway; her expression softened.

Sophy's posture changed immediately, becoming more fluid as she turned to whoever was in the doorway. "Hello, Renni," she said with a blinding smile, tone lighter. "I was just trying to explain the importance of good quality new shoes for the team. Rosa doesn't seem to understand the vital partnership of our sponsors. We're such a fledgling club, big deals like this will keep us all employed."

Renni's gaze flicked back to Rosa. Her lips compressed as she frowned. Having been at her job for a couple of decades, working for several different clubs, she was more than adept at her job and understood her part of the industry very well.

"I can't speak for the other guys," he shrugged, "but my contract is very clear about my cleats. I choose what is best."

Sophy stiffened. She'd clearly been expecting him to take her side of the argument, or at least understand what a wonderful thing she was trying to do.

This wasn't the first time he'd witnessed her trying to bully one of the professional support staff into doing what she wanted them to do. He'd also overheard her complain to Smith about how the staff were ignorant and incompetent.

"We'll continue this discussion later," Sophy said to Rosa.

"The players aren't going to go for this," Rosa said.

"It's your job to see that they do." Sophy's voice was so acidic it ate at the sweet overtone she tried to coat it with before leaving the room.

Rosa sighed.

"You alright?"

She glanced up at him and smiled. "Of course I am, just trying to avert the coming chaos.

She is so set on what she thinks is best for the club, with no sense on what is actually right for the team. Since she got here, the harmony of the club staff has been slipping and becoming discordant. No one can say anything to Smith. He's got a soft spot for her and backs her, no matter what."

Renni nodded, he'd been subjected to it himself already. "Do you want me to talk to Smith?"

"I can handle it myself, but thanks for your concern," Rosa said. "Anyway, we're here to discuss the health of your cleats; let's focus on that." Rosa got back to business, explaining the treatments she had applied to the footwear.

THREE

"CAPTAIN," PIA SAID AS she entered the precinct captain's office after her shift.

Looking up, Joseph Bergeron nodded and pointed to a chair in front of his desk, then slid his desk phone between them, put it on speaker, and dialed.

She closed the door and settled as the voice of her GPSA squad lead, Tamara Cole, filled the office from the phone's speaker. "Good afternoon, Captain Bergeron."

"Jensen is here, too," he said.

"Perfect. I read through your report this morning, Pia. Everything looks as though it's still going smoothly except for this one comment you had about a local robbery ring."

"Yes. For the most part the local paranormal community maintains a low profile and police themselves." Pia glanced at Captain Bergeron. "Two local detectives have been investigating an ongoing string of robberies in one of the more affluent areas of the city. Most-ly sports-related paraphernalia has been taken from the homes. Particular and valuable."

Bergeron grunted. "Very capable detectives."

"I'm not questioning their ability to do their jobs. But not being part of the paranormal community, they wouldn't know what signs to look for."

"Such as?" Bergeron prompted.

"I wouldn't stick my nose in this, except that they're frustrated, too. They don't know I've started covering their case, and I plan to keep it that way." She glanced at Bergeron again.

"But?" Cole said.

"They've arrested multiple pairs of human suspects who could be traced back to the scenes. And the detectives are aware they're missing who is organizing the ring. They're also missing the fact that a shifter is involved. By the time I get to the scenes, the scents are so faint I can't distinguish anything other than the fact that a shifter has been on the premises of the robbery within a few days before the event. I haven't been to all of the locations, just the last couple."

"And you're sure it's the same group?" Cole asked.

"My detectives believe so." Bergeron said.

"I do too." Pia added.

"Captain Bergeron, if you are in agreement, I think Pia should investigate further. Don't break cover. The detectives don't need to know the particulars at this point. Not unless you deem it absolutely necessary."

"They wouldn't like someone poking through their case files, questioning their ability."

"No one is questioning them, sir." Pia said.

Bergeron held up a hand and nodded. "I understand that. From their perspective, it wouldn't be seen that way."

"Well, as a traffic cop, I'd have no business sticking my nose in their case files anyway. We have to decide when and how to bring some of your people into what I'm really here for, Captain," Pia said.

"Pia will continue to report directly to you," Cole said. "Keep me in the loop. If shifters are behind this and they turn out to be dangerous, I need to know if and when to send in backup. Captain, you and I can discuss an integration timeline later."

Pia sat up straighter. "I thought my team were all on assignments."

"They are. Deep cases, like yours. So, I'll need time to tap other GPSA agents."

Pia grinned. "Agent Perenga owes me a favor after the take down at the Port of Montreal."

Bergeron grunted again. "That was good work. A lot of arrests that night." He turned to Pia. "Do you think the cases are linked?"

"No." She said, voice clipped at the assumption what one group did, they all did. The only difference between the hidden world and the not hidden world was ability. People were still people. Assholes and saints alike. Bergeron seemed to be old school in his general attitudes about things.

He shrugged. "My job is to make sure my precinct runs efficiently. And if that means Jensen has to do her shifty thing to help put away criminals then I'll do what I can to enable that. I just want to make sure it's kept under wraps."

Pia bristled. "We're not in the habit of exposing ourselves to the public on purpose."

"Yeah, well, despite events down at the port being some really good police work, the newspapers picked up reports of creatures sighted at the scene—very large creatures—and it's made things messy for us trying to keep the police force on solid footing with the local community."

Pia recalled the events of that night. "My colleague had no choice, he had to shift into his beast form. If he hadn't, the leader of that human trafficking ring would have escaped."

Bergeron crossed his arms. "I'm not debating that. The point is, he was seen. And on top of working hard to keep the peace and safety of our community, we also have to do double time to ensure a clean reputation with the public."

Cole's voice cut in from the speaker phone. "Captain, it is in our own best interest to maintain our secret. If we are exposed, it is usually unavoidable. We do our best to run interference afterward. There's only so much we can do if we're not granted access to all of the security camera footage in the aftermath."

"Still. I have my department's image to consider."

"Understood," Cole said, "if we are in agreement, Pia will follow up on potential paranormal involvement with your robbery case, and I'll send out feelers in case you need to call in help. And Jensen, you *will* call in help if things get sticky."

Pia hesitated. "Yes, Ma'am."

"Pia."

"I will."

She glanced up to see Bergeron studying her as he ended the call with Agent Cole. "You've been here almost a year. I've seen you in action and I'm still trying to wrap my head around this."

She shrugged, then stood to leave. "Aside from outside influences instigating the events at the port, Montreal has been pretty quiet. Maybe it will stay that way."

He nodded. "I hope so, too. I'll talk to Cole later about when to bring my people in on your world. I don't want to cause a schism in the precinct." He glanced at his watch and smiled. "You're off to the game tonight?"

Pia grinned. "Absolutely."

"I heard you ticketed Diaz this morning."

"I sure did."

Bergeron shook his head, grin widening. "I'll get the latest robbery case files for you. See you tomorrow."

RENNI SWIPED THE SWEAT from his forehead as he surveyed the field, adjusting the band holding his unruly hair out of his eyes.

Dios, I need to cut my hair.

While the humidity dragged at his lithe muscles, the adrenaline kept him alert.

He tucked an errant strand behind his ear as he jogged left, maintaining his position, watching the flow of the ball and his dark green and gold clad team. Waiting for an opening. Moving constantly, aware of the positions of his teammates, he noted Wong moving toward the goal. Harry Loader moved to support him.

Opposing players began to cluster; a few slid into place to cover Loader, the powerhouse. Wong slipped by.

Renni's head swung toward where the action was. Omar Naas punted the ball between players and broke free of the cluster racing up the side. Renni pivoted, darting forward to provide support as Naas ran toward Loader, then dodged another incoming player.

Renni shouted. An instant later his left foot extended to receive the pass as he ran forward. Wong moved in around Loader, who still had several players guarding him as he moved toward Renni.

Renni sprinted, putting several yards between himself and his own mark. He glanced up, found Wong, and passed.

Seconds later there was a deliberate *thunk* and sharp hiss as Wong headed the ball past the keeper's outstretched hand.

Wong shot Renni a wide grin as Loader, Naas and several other players jumped on Wong in celebration.

Another goal.

Renni was satisfied that this new team was holding their own against the older, more established Montreal team.

He had just enough time to sweep an eye across the spectators, wondering.

Is she here?

Constable Jensen had said she had tickets to the game. There were far too many faces to pick her out of the crowd.

He chuckled to himself. He didn't even know if she supported his team or the rival city team.

No matter. It was a beautiful play.

He'd see her at the pub later that night, as he'd told her he would.

He moved back into position, ready to anticipate the rival response. Motivated to regain control of the game, the opposing players came in hard and fast. He'd played some of the toughest players in Britain and the nimblest in Europe. He could handle himself.

This was why the club had brought him in.

He ushered thoughts of the lovely constable to the back of his mind as he concentrated on the field, watchful for the next opening.

FOUR

THE NIGHT AIR WAS heavy with the heady perfume of tiger lilies in bloom and thick tree greenery. A perfect night for a walk.

Pia skipped up the stone steps of the *Chatton Noir* that was just a few blocks from her apartment. Laughter and raucous conversation spilled out as she pulled the heavy brass handle of the pub's oak and glass door open and strode inside.

In the low light, she recognized some of the familiar faces of her coworkers amid plenty of unfamiliar smiles, all having a good time. The scent of alcohol infused the two-centuries-old establishment, saturating the old wooden beams, scuffed floors, and scarred tables.

Her squad lead, Tamara Cole, had texted her during the game, setting another meeting for the next morning.

Pia sighed. Another update on the local shifter community. Which, aside from the recent events down at the Port of Montreal, was usually pretty quiet. Pia had been called in as back up to help bring down a human trafficking ring that fellow Global Paranormal Security Agency agent, Carson Perenga, had tracked to Montreal from New York, involving a crime boss from Quebec City. It was a pretty wrecked case. She was glad to jump into the fray and get her claws dirty when things went wild.

Lately, she'd been getting restless. It felt good to be back in action with other agents that were on her level. She missed her squad. The girls. All spread out fulfilling missions. It felt like forever since they'd been on a case all together.

She missed the sense of teamwork and belonging she'd begun to enjoy for the first time in her life.

Pia swallowed. She shouldn't complain. She'd asked to take this year-long post so that she could be closer to her dad in his last months. She'd been with him to the end, then numbly settled his estate. Having put everything in order long before Pia's arrival, there wasn't a ton to do. Still, she hadn't been able to talk herself into selling his mountain-home cottage. Her brain constantly skittered away from the idea whenever the subject came up with the estate lawyer.

She'd always loved being in the city when she came out this way to visit her father, but now, since his passing.... There was no longer anything tying her here and she was looking forward to moving on.

Well, except her long-time friend and occasional lover, Erin, who was supposed to meet Pia for a drink in lieu of the game she'd bailed on earlier that evening.

Just a couple more months. Pia hoped she'd be able to dive right back into her GPSA squad again once back on site. She tipped her drink, swishing the ice around the glass, and took a sip.

With the other women of her unit, she'd finally started to feel like she'd found a place where she belonged.

The eternal outsider.

Pia snorted at the self-pity threatening to drag her down.

Better ways to spend my energy.

She quickly flipped her thoughts back to that evening's soccer game as highlights flashed across the screen suspended on the wall adjacent to the bar.

A solid game with plenty of tension as each team battled for dominance. She smiled watching the replay of Renni Diaz's late game equalizer. The impact of his foot, at the perfect angle, set the ball soaring over the heads of several defenders, forcing the goalkeeper into acrobatics, his fingers outstretched, but an inch shy of stopping it from striking the back of the net.

Beautiful.

More camera shots of Renni Diaz kissing the gold trimmed badge of his dark green jersey as his team members ran up to lift him in bear hugs.

The sports cast switched to golf, and she quickly abandoned her place in front of the screen, turning to see a couple of fellow officers, James Hare and Kala Maliki, enter the pub. Picking up her drink, she wandered toward them.

"Jim, Kala, congratulations on the recent break-through with your case. That was months of work. Can I get you both a drink?" She grinned, shaking their hands as a cloud of Kala's coconut shampoo surrounded her.

Jim nodded, returning the smile. "Appreciated, thanks." Traces of his wife's perfume tickled her nose.

Kala shook Pia's hand, though her smile was less enthusiastic. "Thanks. We caught the thieves connected to the robbery ring, but my gut says we don't have everyone involved."

Jim shrugged. "We'll keep looking, but the bulk of the case is solved. Some of the stolen goods were recovered, most is long gone on the black market. Who knew sports memorabilia was such a hot commodity?"

Pia nodded. "A major hurdle. Enjoy the break." She smiled at both of them, then signaled the bartender that she was picking up the tab for the partners and wandered toward the back of the pub to see who was playing pool while she waited for Erin to show up or bail again.

It was part of Pia's job on this particular mission as a Global Paranormal Security Agency agent to remain as up to date as possible of the ongoing cases around her, if she were needed to intervene when someone more than human was required. She also had to be careful of meddling. She wasn't an investigator in this police department. Only the precinct captain and certain members of his chain of command knew of her secret; that she was a shifter, embedded in the local police department, on the look-out for paranormal criminals crossing the border into Canada as an attempt to escape the law.

Well, Canada didn't want criminals, human or paranormal, any more than anyone else did. And Montreal was one of the perfect locations for her to do the job.

The member of the robbery ring that eluded Hare and Maliki was a paranormal. She was sure of it. Pia had smelled the distinct scent of shifter when she'd visited the more recent location herself—incognito, of course, before reporting to the precinct Captain.

Her phone buzzed.

Sorry P, Dave called in sick. Have to cover his shift. Promise to make it up to you later ;)

Pia sighed.

OK, don't take any shit.

Erin replied.

Never do. They know who's boss
of the place. Kiss-kiss.

Pia tucked her phone into her back pocket
and took another sip of her drink.

After a few moments watching active games
of pool, Pia glanced up as the front door
opened. The tenor of the room changed as
Renni Diaz walked through the door.

Her heart stopped.

Surprise and delight rippled through the
crowd, and some of the patrons approached
Renni, congratulating him on his goal. He
made several friendly exchanges as his eyes
swept the pub, landing on her.

With a grin, he strode straight to where Pia
stood, at the arch dividing the main room from
the billiard room.

By the time he reached her, her heart had
kick-started again.

She drew in a sharp breath of his bergamot
and black pepper aftershave, swallowing the
urge to purr as her inner kitty recognized his
personal scent.

Goddess, he is hot.

The suit was long gone, replaced with faded jeans and a black tee that draped his body, following the lines of muscle. Her eyes swept the fully exposed tattoos of his sculpted arms downward, skipping over the rows of beads encircling his wrist, to the strong, lean hands, stopping at the bright pink stamp adorning the back of the right.

"A pony?"

"Jealous?" The low, delicious drawl of his Spanish accent was like fingertips ghosting up her spine inviting her into his sphere.

"Very." She grinned. "What tattoo parlor did you pick that up from?"

He laughed. "My neighbor, and I'm pretty sure that ink is just as permanent as all the rest. Takes days to wash off."

She liked the way his eyes twinkled in the low light. "Drink?"

"Soda water," he said with a nod.

She quirked a brow and approached the bar, relaying the order along with another of her own.

Drinks in hand, they took up residence at a recently vacated bar table.

"So, I didn't expect to see you here," Pia said, climbing up on to the stool, hooking her toes under the foot brace to keep them from swinging.

Renni settled onto his stool, one foot propped, the toes of his other rested on the peanut-dusted floor. He shrugged. "I said I'd come." He sipped from his glass, the corners of his eyes crinkling over the rim at her.

"Still." She wasn't letting it go. Was this normal for globally adored sports stars? He was the only one she'd ever seen walk through the door of this place since she'd arrived. Then again, it wasn't like she came here all *that* often.

A couple of new arrivals came by to say hello to Renni, and politely acknowledged her.

"Let's start again, shall we? Pia Jensen," she said, offering her hand.

He shook it, his fingers lingering, much as they had that morning during their first exchange. "Renni Diaz." He grinned.

"How often do you come here?"

His eyes were already locked on her face. His lips quirked, drawing her attention.

Very nice lips, indeed.

"Not often—only once or twice, in fact. I attend a lot of charity functions and get out into the community as much as I can."

How did she not know this? That will teach her for avoiding social media like the plague and keeping her head buried in work.

"The city, in partnership with local sports clubs, has been working hard to raise its profile, along with that of the local police, so I see a number of these folks at different event circuits," he said. "Maybe I'll run into you at one soon."

"Not likely." She smiled without elaborating. Now that she thought about it, she did remember the captain looking for officers to attend public events. As a low-profile agent, she managed to slide clean of any public facing obligations.

She eyed him as her first impressions from that morning began to crumble along the edges. Maybe there was hope that he wasn't the arrogant asshole she'd started to believe he was. "Not afraid of parking that expensive car of yours in a neighborhood like this?"

"With all these police officers around? Besides, it's a beautiful night, so I left her snug at home and took my motorbike instead."

Motorbike?

Oh. Oh no. No.

Her teeth caught her lower lip as the image of him straddling a motorcycle slid through her lusty brain.

"What kind of bike?" She cringed inwardly at the eager tone of her voice. She swallowed and considered him. "Let me guess. A Ninja? No. Ducati. Surely not a Harley?"

"Everyone's got a Harley. Victory Gunner. I like to go for things that are different." He grinned.

Hooked, she sighed.

Dangerous. She wriggled on her stool to adjust her posture, trying to ignore her growing arousal.

Smiling eyes, lips that could make a girl stare for hours, a skilled athlete with a killer physique, *and* a motorbike. She licked her lips to ensure she wasn't drooling on the table and sipped her drink.

"Would you... like to go for a ride?"

Her gaze snapped to his twinkling eyes.

Oh my god yes!!

It was an effort to glance around the busy pub and force a nonchalant shrug. "Maybe later."

He sipped his drink, eyes on her face. She had the distinct impression he saw right through her attempt at mild interest.

"So." She decided to change the subject. "You're from Argentina, right? How did you find your first winter in Montreal?" Pia knew damned well he was from Argentina, she'd followed his career on and off for years.

Renni chuckled. "Unexpectedly crisp. I didn't know nose hair could freeze like that. I'd imagine it's nothing for you? Did you grow up here?"

"Upstate New York. Yes, I'm acclimated. Don't love the cold, but I survive it."

"Really? What brings you to Montreal?"

"My dad. I came to spend his last months with him before his passing. He moved to the Laurentians north of the city years ago, so I spent my summers here. He's the one that molded my love of soccer, signing me up with local leagues when I was a kid. He followed your career. He would have been thrilled to have met you."

Renni's expression had turned serious. "Has he been gone long?"

"He passed last spring." Dropping her gaze to her drink, her thumb slid across the rim as grief rippled through her.

"I'm sorry." He studied her a moment longer then smiled. "Do you still play?"

She shook her head.

"Too bad," he said. "I could challenge you to a game. You learn a lot about a person by how they play."

She glanced back up and smiled. Changing the subject she said, "you've played for the biggest teams around the world; why here?"

He shrugged, accepting the return to less fragile topics. "I reached the top of my career and looked around me and decided it was a good time to start giving back to the sport that had brought me so much." He smiled.

Pia's heart fluttered at the genuine appreciation that filled his expression.

"New league, new team, new challenges."

His aura oozed charm and mesmerism. She was falling into his eyes and her kitty was on board.

This, she couldn't afford.

Keep it simple Pia. Maybe have some fun but keep your distance. Just a couple more months and you're moving on.

Besides, soccer stars and undercover paranormals were probably a bad mix.

Definitely a bad mix. No 'probably' about it.

He was just so goddess-damned hot, and charming.

Even if they did end up in bed, it wasn't like he was going to find out about her kitty side.

Still, she'd have to tread carefully.

Maybe now was a good time to go for that ride.

Or walk away Pia.

Kitty growled.

"Shall we go for that ride?" She asked, pushing the rest of her drink aside.

"Absolutely." Renni's teeth flashed in his dark face. His eyes twinkled again as he stood to follow Pia out of the pub.

She spotted the sleek cruiser nestled at an angle between two parked cars.

He led her to it. "Have you ridden before?"

"Yeah," she breathed, curling her fingers to stop herself from stroking the leather seat. "I have a Shadow in storage back home. She's much smaller than this."

Renni pulled a helmet from one of the saddlebags, handing it to her before going around to the other and retrieving his own. He dipped into his pocket, pulling keys out before swinging a long leg over the bike.

Pia's eyes locked on his ass as he settled onto the bike after releasing the kickstand.

She fastened the helmet on her head.

Get a grip Pia—yourself—not his ass!

She sighed, rubbing her palms down the thighs of her jeans.

It's probably a good thing you didn't finish your second drink. What's wrong with you?

The bike roared to life, calling to her, then settled into a rumble.

After a few seconds, Pia realized she'd been purring in response and quickly cut it out. She couldn't freak Renni out on their first... what was this? Not a date? Meet up?

She shrugged and smiled when he turned and signaled for her to get on behind him. It was hard to ignore the intimacy of sitting with him between her legs. Her eyes swept the strong muscle of his back under the soft fabric of his tee shirt.

Pia usually drove her own bike, fingers curled around the handles. She hesitated, before resting her hands on her thighs, letting the short backrest settle in the small of her back.

Renni twisted, glancing down at her left hand, then reached back and pulled it around his waist, her palm on his stomach.

Leaning forward, she slid the other around and linked her fingers together. The heat of his body radiated toward her.

Goddess, he smelled good.

As soon as Pia's fingers laced across his abdomen, Renni gunned the engine and took off. Focusing on the road and traffic suddenly required a little more effort. He'd gone hard the instant Pia's hands slid across his belly and settled on the edge of his belt buckle.

He'd certainly appreciated her enthusiasm and clear love of bikes. Most people refused, on the rare occasions he had offered anyone a ride.

He navigated the narrow streets, easing between pedestrians streaming through the city center even at this hour. He turned onto the nearest highway ramp, merged with the lighter traffic, and once in the farthest lane over, he let her loose.

Freedom.

The roar of the engine and the howl of the wind enveloped them in a sound barrier, drowning out everything else.

When Renni was on his bike, he let himself become part of it—or it, part of him. There was just the road and the wind. And tonight, Constable Pia Jensen.

From the second she'd strode up to his car that morning, he knew he wanted her.

The imperial glare she'd cast down on him as she'd handed him the ticket.

The shock of his presence at the pub, and her gradual softening.

Studying her face while they chatted over their drinks, he'd been pulled in by her subtle magnetism. His instinct drove him to offer her a ride.

He'd been rewarded with the shutters falling away and a ray of sunshine lighting her face despite her nonchalant answer.

He wanted to kiss her right then and there.

The slight upturn of her small nose was adorable. He longed to slide his fingers through her thick dark hair. And the way she stood—the way she moved was as though she had far too much energy for her small frame.

Despite his resistance, he hadn't felt that kind of overwhelming impulse to kiss anyone since he'd discovered kissing.

After a while, her arms slid tighter around his waist, and he felt her cheek against his shoulder blade. His heart pounded in his chest, unable to clear the goofy grin on his face. He was tempted to spirit her away to his house and spend the next week getting to know her.

Instead, he headed off the highway, guiding the motorcycle up Mount Royal, where they parked and walked the paths in quiet conversation.

"I've seen this place in the tourist guides, but I've never been up here myself." Pia said.

Renni looked down into her smiling face. "I come here now and then." He gestured toward the path curving around Mount Royal Chalet. "I like to come here for a bit of perspective," he said as the path opened to a large viewing terrace. The city's skyscrapers rose up like illuminated matrixes adorned with glittering gemstones just beyond the balustrade and treetops. The St. Lawrence River shimmered under the moonlight behind the buildings and streetlights.

"Oh, it's beautiful!" She breathed, hand to chest as she walked toward the stone handrail.

Renni turned his back on the cityscape and sat on the ledge letting his eyes take in all that was Pia. "I prefer *this* view."

Her eyes flicked to him in surprise. Her smile turned shy and her attention returned to the island of Montreal spread out before her. She laughed.

"You look like a queen surveying her lands."

Pia laughed, "Would you be my consort?" She regarded him from the corner of her eye.

"Not your king?"

"Hmm," she twisted her body toward him, considering him with a grin. "You do have a shiny steed and flowing locks. Any man wishing to step up to the honor of being *my* king would need to be noble of heart, brave of deed, and hot as hell."

Renni grinned back, "I'm hot as hell already, so brave and noble will need some work."

Pia laughed, full and throaty.

The sound rolled through him, urging him to reach for her. He crossed his arms, unable to chase away the sense of light and laughter she inspired in him.

After a while she said, "I see what you mean. Being up here, seeing the city like this, it does give you a different perspective. From the individual to the community."

Finally, Renni stood and enjoyed the cityscape next to Pia. He couldn't stop himself from periodically looking down into her lovely oval face.

Without meaning to, he found himself closer to her.

It had been difficult to focus on anything other than Pia all day. There was something in the way she looked at him. She *really* looked at him. Like there was more to him than what he presented to the world.

This both terrified and thrilled him at once.

Intriguing.

He leaned forward, hands splayed on the balustrade. "Community has become my focus. To strengthen any community I come into in a positive way," he said.

She turned her face toward him. The city lights caught in her irises, turning them a luminescent gold, making her seem 'other' for a split second.

Her hand slid over his. "That, Renni, is noble of heart."

A heart that quickened at the slightest of her touches; something he had not experienced in a very long time.

"If I am to try to fulfill this lofty quest, I should get some beauty rest. It's not easy being hot as hell."

She laughed again, following him back toward his motorcycle so he could drive her home.

He offered to take her back to her place.

"I like the walk." She insisted as she got off the bike outside of the *Chatton Noir*. "Thanks for the ride. I really enjoyed it."

Renni released the kickstand, then got off the motorcycle and removed his helmet.

Pia removed hers, then handed it back to him. His eyes caressed her glowing expression before he secured the spare helmet back in the saddlebag.

"Since I let you buy me a drink, you'll have to let me take you to dinner," he said once finished.

Surprise flashed across her face, followed by uncertainty as tension drew her shoulders up a fraction.

"No strings attached."

She visibly relaxed again, considering him. "No strings attached?"

He shook his head. "Absolutely none." And he meant it, no matter how much he wanted her. His eyes slipped to her lips, wanting to taste them. He sat down on the side of the bike's seat and crossed his arms.

"No expectations. At all." She said, curiosity drawing her toward him.

Renni smiled.

She stepped closer yet again, as though testing. "What if I wanted to kiss you?"

He grinned. "Then there would be a kiss." His pulse accelerated. He tucked his hands further to stop himself from reaching for her. To stop himself from pulling her down onto his lap so that he could explore her mouth.

"Just like that."

He nodded.

Another step brought her so close she stood between his knees, looking down into his face, studying him.

"It would be just a kiss." He said simply.

She shifted her weight to one leg as she regarded him, hand on hip. "That sounds like a challenge."

"Is it?" He couldn't stop his grin from widening.

Her curiosity was written all over her face as her eyes locked on his lips. Every thought evident for him to read. He held his breath, waiting to see if she'd rise to the challenge or shy away.

Her eyes flicked back to his. Her hunger unmistakable.

Still, he waited, fingers twitching, hidden beneath his still-crossed arms.

"Just a kiss. No expectations. No strings." Her voice was little more than a breath as she took that final step, thighs pressed between his, as he remained seated on the edge of his bike.

"Yes. I should warn you, once you kiss me, you'll want more." He'd gone hard at her returned proximity and the knowledge that she wanted a kiss as much as he did. He was going to need an ice-cold shower when he got home.

Amusement flickered across her features, her eyes flashing at the challenge issued. "We'll see," she said.

He looked up into her beautiful face. Full lips parted, eyes sparkling. Her short stature brought her almost in line with him.

She leaned toward him, her hair falling so that it framed both their faces.

He inhaled as the scent of her hair enveloped them with vanilla and oranges.

Other than tilting his face up to her, he remained still.

Pia's left hand rose, tentative. Hesitant. Her fingers ghosted the side of his face as she slid her lips across his.

Christ, she was sweet. His pulse accelerated; his head lightened.

Intoxicating.

Her lips tested his. After a moment, when it seemed she would pull away, the tip of his tongue flicked against her lower lip, drawing her further in.

She followed. Her right hand sought his shoulder as she deepened the kiss, exploring him, deeper and deeper until he thought she just might crawl onto his lap.

He wished she would. He wanted to fill his hands with her ass, bury his face in her breasts, take her home for different kind of ride.

He broke the kiss, easing the retreat with a tender nibble. Drawing a deep breath, he smiled up into her face.

She blinked, focusing on his lips, slowly straightening her spine. Her hand jerked away from his shoulder like he'd burned her.

"It's all right, *cara*. Just a kiss," he said, despite the fact he was sure his balls would explode on the drive home.

At the sound of his gruff voice, she looked as though she wanted to devour him again.

"Dinner?" he asked.

She drew a deep breath, licking her lips as she considered him.

Fuck, she was going to be the death of him.

Pia cocked a brow, her smile widened. "I'll think about it." She turned to go.

"I don't have your number." He prompted, pulling his cell from his pocket.

Turning back, she reached for the device, added her number and held it out for him.

His eyes held hers. His fingers trailed over hers as he retrieved his phone.

She turned to go again. This time when she turned back, her eyes glittered mischief under the dull streetlamp. Her hand waved toward the bike. "Oh, and this time, I'll let you off with a warning Mr. Diaz. Watch your speed, sir."

He laughed, "Yes Ma'am. Kids and seniors have places to go, too."

"That's right." She winked at him, and this time when she turned to go, she didn't look back.

FIVE

RENNI WALKED INTO THE training facility, finding his way through the complex by muscle memory. His mind was preoccupied with the feisty, bright-eyed traffic cop—who he'd not seen since he dropped her off outside the pub several nights past. Her patrol car hadn't been parked along his route to the training complex, where he was due to meet to discuss another upcoming publicity event.

As he swung the door open, several figures looked up. The club manager, Daniel Smith; Smith's personal assistant, Sophy Khienak; and Renni's agent, Brian Gerrard. The latter stepped forward with a smile and an extended hand.

Smith scowled, as usual.

Sophy's eyes were glued to Renni and his agent.

"Let's get started," she prompted, as though they'd been chitchatting for a quarter hour, when they'd barely exchanged a few words.

Smith cleared his throat, shuffled his papers, and frowned at Renni until he settled down.

The two stood up before them and the hair on the back of Renni's neck began to rise. He wasn't going to like whatever they were going to say. Their demeanor and fidgety actions felt more like some kind of contract break than a publicity planning event.

"Sophy has come up with a new idea." Smith said, then moved aside.

Sophy flipped a long blond curl over her shoulder, squared her posture by shuffling her high heeled shoes closer together, and plastered a wide, red-lipped smile on her face.

"Since the Global Trophy is stopping here for its first part of the tour across North America, I'm proposing a pre-unveiling event at the gala. I've been helping the club events team, in partnership with the other clubs and the league representatives, to plan the Montreal gala. It's perfect! All of the most important people in the World Association, the North American league, local big wigs, international media—everyone will be there."

Renni suppressed a sigh.

"An auction." Her sudden, forced enthusiasm was thrown at them.

He waited, brows rising.

"Auction of what?" Gerrard asked.

"Renni."

"No." Renni said.

"Just listen." She encouraged.

Renni began shaking his head. He didn't like where this was going already.

"Time. A night of your time. That's all." Smith said.

"Like, a date if the winner is a woman. Or a guys' night if the winner is a man."

"No." Renni said again before Gerrard could open his mouth. He sat forward on his seat, planting both feet on the floor, palms rubbing together as he stared from one to the other.

"Care to elaborate?" Smith said.

Renni glanced at Gerrard, who shrugged.

"I do coordinated publicity events with other team members and other organizations. It's never about me as in individual. I thought you understood that." His eyes leveled on Sophy. "I said this the last time you ambushed me and suggested a similar event. My presence is about raising the profile of the club within the league and raising the profile of the league on the continent."

Smith's glare shot to Sophy, his brows drawn.

Sophy's cheeks were bright spots on her pale face, her red lips thinned. She couldn't argue the statement that he'd repeated almost word for word. Her proposal was almost the same proposal, just word for word altered.

"We can still work with the general idea." Gerrard offered. "Take the focus off Renni and put it back on the club. Time with the team—a friendly game of sorts?"

"Harder to organize and not enough time to set it up at this point in the season," Smith said.

"What if we just keep the auction idea, insert an object, and add more players and organizations."

Which is exactly where Renni thought this meeting was going to go in the first place.

Why the hell was Sophy so focused on singling him out? He'd made it very clear that's not the kind of profile he wanted. Renni was a team player. His agent understood that.

Renni had done heavy solo marketing contracts earlier in his career, and while it made him a lot of money, that was no longer how he wanted to be presented. It created too much drama and invited trouble. That kind of focus generated team divisions instead of team unity.

"What kind of object can we procure as donation for the auction?" Gerrard asked. "Renni's already donated most of his earned hardware to previous charity events back home." He glanced from Renni to Smith. "Why don't we ask the club to donate something? Season ticket packages or something. And approach the players to see if they'd like to participate. Let everyone choose something."

Sophy still hadn't answered. She stood ramrod straight, clearly not liking that her proposal had been shot down and altered. She didn't seem to like the compromise offered.

Renni sighed. He wasn't going to worry about it. She'd been told before, and he was no longer going to allow people to try to manipulate or force him into situations he didn't like. He'd done that a lot early on in his career, too.

"The Gala is what—next week? Renni's already scheduled to attend." Gerrard said.

"This weekend." Sophy said, voice tight.

Gerrard's brows rose. "That's pretty soon for an event that hasn't been planned yet. There's no time for advertising. Can you pull it off?"

The color of Sophy's cheeks deepened as her eyes narrowed on Gerrard. "My plan would have been simple to pull together with plenty of time." She tossed her hair again. "Everyone we'd need to attend will already be at the planned gala. We'd just announce it as a surprise auction before the unveiling. The process would have taken five minutes tops for an evening of Renni's time, which would have raised a lot of money for the club's charity."

Smith nodded.

Gerrard shrugged. "You're planning it. I'm just here to make sure Renni's comfortable with the proposal. And as the proposal stands, he isn't comfortable."

"I'll have to rework the plan." Sophy said through clenched jaw. "Although it would be simpler if Renni could just give a little bit of his time for one evening."

Renni frowned at Sophy.

He stood, glanced at his watch and said, "I'm going to change for practice." He looked to Smith, patted Gerrard on the shoulder, and left the meeting room without another glance at Sophy.

She wasn't an events planner. She was the manager's personal assistant. He sighed. Had the proposed idea even been brought to the executive and publicity team? He doubted it. Likely, Sophy had pushed the idea on Smith to get his backing to take it to the board and put herself in charge.

No wonder she looked so pissed when Renni refused again. She was banking on his cooperation. She was trying to set him up as her leverage with the executive team.

Ambitious.

Renni respected ambition.

He loathed underhanded manipulation.

Carlos and his father invaded his thoughts. He shoved them away again. Less than twenty minutes in a meeting and he was on edge. He finished changing, lost in his memories as his teammates wandered around him, then headed out to the field to put his mind where it needed to be.

PAWS LIGHT ON THE pavement, Pia prowled in her panther form. Her inner kitty was eager to stretch her muscles and run and jump. She had work to do. The sleek black fur on her forelegs and paws glimmered under a random street-light as she slid between the shadows.

She was revisiting the neighborhood where the most recent robbery had taken place, determined to help Jim and Kala close their case for good. They were good investigators, but sometimes it was hard to link missing pieces when paranormals were involved, and Pia was sure there were, this time. Otherwise, she'd have kept her nose out of their case files.

She stood, head raised, tasting the air, eyes closed.

So many smells to tease apart to find the right one. Especially now with time passing.

Nothing. She moved closer, careful to avoid the properties where she now knew dogs lived. A couple of the other break-ins had been in this same area. Indoor cats stared at her from their illuminated windows. They could sense her presence. She wasn't there to aggravate them. She glanced at a tabby pacing its small window. It couldn't be helped. She kept going, on to the property she was targeting.

The houses were almost as large as her slouching three-story downtown apartment building. The neighborhood was affluent, with automatic sprinkler systems embedded everywhere in the sprawling lawns. She hated those.

Trotting past another multi-car garage, she wove her way around Jacuzzi tubs, skirted in-ground pools and outdoor stone kitchens and found a shadowed spot. Under a leafy lilac bush with its blooms long gone, she watched the occupants of the house through their well-lit floor-to-ceiling windows and patio doors. Normally, they'd have privacy with the high fencing and lush landscaping. Anyone standing in the back yard had a full view into the private lives of the house dwellers as they moved from room to room.

What is it like to be so at ease among such luxury?

Like it was nothing. To be as comfortable in the cavernous house as she was in her small downtown apartment, without thought to its cost and maintenance.

Renni Diaz must live in a house like this.

Do I truly envy that lifestyle?

With the amount of housework required? She cringed. Then again, anyone able to afford a house like that could also afford housekeepers.

Clearly their lifestyle had its complications. This family had been targeted for their valuable possessions.

A light came on in an upper room with a small Italianate balcony jutting from a set of French doors. Its occupant moved through the room, unbuttoning his shirt, tossing it on to a bed. He wandered back and forth, exchanging clothing, settling jewelry and other trinkets on a dresser top.

Some sort of collectible item, along with money and jewelry had been stolen from this house. Sports paraphernalia prized by its owner, unrecovered, likely sold on the black market.

She watched as he retrieved his suit jacket and placed it and his tie and shoes back in his walk-in closet, visible from her vantage point. The light went off again, as did several others on the main floor. The kitchen light dimmed, remaining on. The household was retiring for the night. With less light being cast on the grounds from the house, it was easier to move unseen across the lawn.

Pia pressed her nose to the grass, scenting again. Adjusting her gaze, she looked for potential clues, invisible to the human eye. She prowled the perimeter studying the ground along the fence. The police had found the shoe prints where the thieves had moved along the edge of the garden. She returned to that spot.

The garden hadn't yet been touched; the shoe prints were still visible. The other targeted properties had the same shoe prints, which were strong clues in the case. What wasn't considered a clue was the canine-like prints that were also present, though sometimes obscured by the shoe tread.

They would be logged as being present, but dismissed as belonging to a neighbor's dog, or a stray. Thieves didn't generally bring their pets to a robbery.

It took a few minutes of intensive seeking. There it was, cut in half by a shoe print, right along the flowerbed lining the fence that ran along the side of the house. Just one. One accidental misstep.

Pia homed in on it, trying to compare it to the others she'd seen, and drew as close to it as she dared without touching her nose directly to it. Her keen vision assessed it for any distinguishing features. The shape of the print was unfamiliar.

She breathed. The faded, lingering scent was the same. All she could tell was that it's tang belonged to an unusual shifter of some kind.

Not wolf. She knew wolf scent. Something else.

The neighborhood grew darker as more household lights flicked off until just the streetlights remained to illuminate the yard. Not that she needed the light to see clearly.

However, Pia was on duty in the morning. Best to make the long run home, write up quick reports for the Captain and agent Cole and then get some sleep.

SIX

PIA YAWNED AS SHE glanced at the speed radar and sipped her coffee. It had taken her a little longer than expected to get home.

It had been a good run.

Glorious to stretch her muscles. Thrilling to stalk and slink among the shadows.

There hadn't been any calls to the precinct about a wild animal spotted, so that was good. Couldn't have the wildlife department on the hunt for her.

This morning, she was back at the same hiding spot where she'd been posted the morning she'd stopped Renni Diaz for speeding.

She smiled, remembering their ride on his Victory Gunner.

And his lips.

She sighed and sipped more coffee.

Speaking of Renni...

She recognized the growl of his sports car before it passed her parked cruiser. The growl eased a fraction, as though he'd taken his foot off the accelerator, then increased again.

She smiled and glanced at the dash clock.

He's probably late again.

Ten minutes later, her phone chimed.

Picking it up, she grinned.

Dinner?

A thrill rippled through her belly as she smiled at her phone, and purring rumbled through her chest.

She let it go unanswered for a while.

Pia giggled. Not only had he actually shown up at the pub and taken her for a ride, he was also actually asking her to dinner, too.

And that kiss!

I still can't believe I kissed Renni Diaz.

He was right though. One kiss and she definitely wanted more, so much more...

Should I?

Dinner with Renni Diaz.

She had to stop the fan girl response. He was a man, like any other. Okay, not quite like any other. A skilled superstar. Incredibly sexy-hot with a killer grin.

It was just a dinner offer. He'd said before there were 'no strings attached'.

Why not?

Why not... She was supposed to be maintaining a low-key persona and dating a high-profile guy was not really low-key, now was it?

But... she'd get to know the man behind the image. There'd been an awful lot about him in the news over the years that had piqued her curiosity. Mostly about his career, though there'd been some other scandal that had hit the news a bunch of years back. Something about connections to crime lords in his hometown that spilled out onto the soccer field at some point. She didn't remember the details; it had been a hectic time in her life with other things to focus on. Rumors, probably.

And of course, he'd always been photographed with a new woman every week. Goddesses, every one of them.

Which Pia was not. Too short to ever be considered glamorous. Too wide in the hip to be elegant.

Maybe she could claim grace? Mostly when she was in her panther form, where absolute muscle control was a given—not that Renni would ever see that part of her. Ever.

When she was her animal self, she was powerful.

Her human self; not so much.

She was low key enough that if some reporter photographed Renni, they'd likely just assume she was a co-worker of sorts. She didn't look anything like the women he was photographed with before.

Still. She had to think about this.

The work came first.

How long had it been since she'd last been out on a date? She could barely remember the last time she'd done anything fun—motorbike ride with Renni aside. And hanging out at Erin's downtown club didn't count.

Probably not since she and her team had spent some quality time together during their road trip that involved deep wilderness hiking in the mountains and wingsuit flying back down again. Wicked fun, but it felt like forever ago. She missed her girls.

The work had always come first, for so long.

This was Renni Diaz. Opportunities like this didn't come by every day. This was a chance to get to know a little bit about who the man behind the talent really was.

And he'd asked her to dinner.

What kind of food does he like? Where would they go?

Reel it back Pia. She tamped down on her rising curiosity. Be cool, not stalker.

Sure.

Was that aloof enough?
The response was instantaneous.

7?

She grinned. Waited. Watched the flow of traffic, adjusted the radio dial, flicked some dust from the radar screen.
Then answered.

Where meet?

Again, instant response.

I'll pick you up.

Her heart fluttered. Motorbike or car? Jeans or skirt?
Did she want him to pick her up at her place?

Pub @ 7

He sent a thumb's up.

Drawing a deep breath, she put the phone down on the seat next to her.

She just had to make sure no one paid any attention to her. She was pretty generic, so, easy-peasy.

A piece-of-shit junk box deafened her as it sped past, causing the radar scanner to flash, confirming it was well over the speed limit.

She threw the cruiser into gear and went after it, lights and siren letting him know she was coming for him.

She blew out a breath. What the hell was she going to wear tonight?

The car pulled over. She called in the plate and then approached the vibrating shit-box. Stepping alongside the driver's window, it descended, spewing a cloud of pot and French rap.

It was barely nine-thirty in the morning. She sighed again as she waited for the yodle to turn off his stereo so he could hear her.

"What the fuck, *esti,* I'm trying to get to work. Just let me off with a warning or my boss is going to fire me for being late again, *tabernak.*"

"Please step out of your car."

It was going to be another fabulous day.

RENNI NAVIGATED HIS CAR along the familiar narrow street, parking in almost the same place he had before. He glanced at the dash. Six-fifty. He checked his hair and teeth in the rear-view mirror, then released his seatbelt and exited the car. He was about to press the lock button on the key fob when the sound of heels on pavement drew his attention.

Pia rounded the corner he'd just passed.

Her smile shone, even at this distance.

She approached, hips swaying with each step, rich dark hair bouncing, catching the golden evening sunlight. "Looks like we're both early."

"Punctuality is important. I wasn't sure where we were going, so I have some flats in my bag." She patted an oversized purse looped over her shoulder.

"Just dinner at my place, unless you have other suggestions?"

"At *your* place?" Her eyes widened.

"Is that alright?"

Uncertainty skittered across her lovely features. Then her smile returned, and she nodded.

"Shall we then?" He turned toward his car and opened the passenger door for her.

She thanked him as she sank down onto the leather seat.

He shut the door, got behind the wheel, and buckled in. As soon as they were pointed toward his house, he struck up the conversation. "Catch many speeders today?"

She turned toward him and grinned "A few. Good thing I had time to shower after my shift. I stank of pot all day." Her nose wrinkled when he glanced at her.

Adorable.

"Well, you smell amazing now."

"Not like pot?"

He shook his head.

"Good. What's for dinner? I'm famished."

"I have steak planned."

"I'm drooling already."

A food lover. *Gracias a Dios*. His shoulders eased as he drove.

He cast her a sideways glance. Her face was in profile as she looked at the passing scene out of her window. She was dressed comfortably in jeans tucked into boots that rose above the knee. Her jacket and purse covered whatever blouse she was wearing.

She had arrived early.

She wore sexy boots, but brought sensible shoes with her.

And she liked steak.

This was already starting out to be a great evening.

RENNI WATCHED AS PIA leaned back in her chair, chewing the last bite of her food, and carefully set her cutlery across her plate.

The steak was gone, a random bit of potato huddled on the side of her plate and the salad bowl still held several lonely spinach leaves and a cherry tomato.

She dabbed her lips with her napkin and sighed.

Renni topped up her wine, earning a smile of thanks as she reached for the glass.

"I had no idea you could cook. I think I have a steak baby, now." She patted her tummy with her free hand.

He laughed, pleased that she had enjoyed his efforts. "We haven't made it to desert yet."

She groaned. "Killing me with kindness."

Pia turned on her chair, crossing her legs to the side. A glint drew Renni's eye to a metallic ball hanging from the chain Pia wore. "Is that a globe?" he nodded toward the necklace in the folds of her loose blouse.

She looked down, scooped up the pendant and grinned, leaning forward so he could see the detail.

He laughed. "A golden soccer ball."

"It has a little shoe charm linked to it," she said, moving it so that he could see it, too.

He rose from his seat and reached out for her hand. "Breath of fresh air?"

She playfully tapped his hand away, laughing. "I'm not so far gone yet I can't get up from a dining room chair."

He smiled and claimed the wine bottle and his glass. She also picked up her glass, and followed him through the darkened patio doors out onto a stone terrace that descended to a lit pool. He stopped before the first step, looking up.

"The city lights block out most of the stars, but you can still see the brightest ones."

"If you drive about forty-five minutes north of here, up into the mountains, the stars are phenomenal," Pia said, joining him to admire the sky. "Up around St. Jerome and St. Hippolyte. Beautiful lake country."

"I will have to go and see this one day." He glanced at her profile. "Would you like to introduce me to these places sometime?"

She turned back to him, brow raised. She sipped her wine, eyes trained on him from over the rim of her glass, then smiled. "Sometime."

Not a commitment, but a step in the right direction.

Her gaze slid from his face to a spot in the yard. Spying a white sphere partially obscured by one of the juniper bushes in the yard, Pia descended the steps to set her glass down on a table wedged between two lounge chairs by the pool. Striding toward the grass on bare feet, she bent to retrieve the soccer ball, tossing it up into the air between her hands. "Can't get enough of the sport, huh?" she teased.

"Never."

She glanced up at Renni's wide grin, illuminated by the wavering pool lights.

Pia raised her knee, letting the ball bounce, then bounced it again with the other, going back and forth.

"I thought you said you didn't play," Renni said, moving closer.

"I don't. Not anymore. Some things you just don't lose from your childhood. While my folks were together, they put me in soccer every summer. After Mom died, Dad used it as a way to provide a sense of normalcy in my life. I'd play with him when I came back to visit after I grew up."

"I lost my mother young, too." He held up his arm, showing her the rosary wrapped around his wrist with a small crucifix dangling against his palm. "This belonged to her."

"I've noticed you wear it on the field."

"At all times."

Renni gave her a light hip bump, setting her off balance, and stole the ball, passing it from foot to foot.

Pia slipped a foot in from behind and punted the ball forward. She moved with lightening reflexes, tipping it past him.

"You're good!" He laughed, seeing she'd won the ball from him, then stepped forward to challenge for it again.

Before he could, she bent and scooped it up from the grass and passed it from hand to hand like a basketball.

"Hey! That's cheating!" a high voice, full of indignation, cried.

Renni and Pia spun in the direction of the neighboring house.

"And that's my ball."

Renni's little neighbor, Ella, sat cross-legged on her small second floor glassed-in balcony with a few dolls.

Pia looked down at the professional grade ball in her hands with pink pony stamps adorning the normally blank spaces.

"Renni gave it to me." Ella said.

"Is it alright if I play with it a little bit?" Pia asked.

"Only if Renni says it's alright."

"It's alright Ella, Pia won't keep it. We'll leave it right here."

"Okay. Are we practicing in the morning?" she rushed on, eyes wide.

"Of course. Every morning, unless you over-sleep."

"Renni teaches us soccer every morning before the bus comes, but since it's summertime, the bus doesn't come, but he teaches us anyway so we can join the new soccer school he's building and be players when we're big too."

Pia blinked then looked at Renni.

At her expression of delightful curiosity at this revelation, he dropped his head, scratching the side of his nose to cover his embarrassment.

"How adorable!" she laughed. To Ella she said, "that sounds very exciting. Shall I just leave your ball right here on the grass?"

"Yes, but you can play with it some more if you want. Are you a soccer player too?"

"I'm a police officer that likes to play soccer sometimes."

"Oh, a police officer! I bet you catch a lot of bad guys!"

He glanced up to see Pia's cheeks pinken as she cast a sidelong glance at Renni who was studying her. "I do," she said with a grin for Ella. "Especially if they drive too fast where they're not supposed to."

Renni chuckled. "Ella, you should take your dolls to bed so that you're not too tired for our lesson in the morning."

"Okay Renni! Good night! Good night Pia police officer!"

They both bid her goodnight as she scooped up her dolls and went inside. Once the door was closed, Renni and Pia looked at each other with new eyes.

"Morning lessons, huh?"

"Morning lessons that make me late for work when there's no school bus to end the lessons, so Pia police officer can chase me down." He stepped toward her, smiling.

"And you're building a soccer school," she said, voice incredulous.

Renni nodded. "It's my thing. Whatever club I'm playing for, I try to talk them into setting up a school for local kids, if they don't already have one. Support the community and encourage the love of sport."

"Not what I expected," she whispered, her eyes studying his face, making him feel as though she could see right inside him. A thrill rippled through him at the idea of being seen for who he really was, which was rare.

He also couldn't shake the threat of vulnerability that came along with it.

Renni held her eyes a moment longer. She was a police officer.

What would she think if she knew about his past? About his father's connections? Would it matter?

He hadn't thought beyond the traffic ticket. What else did *she* get involved in? Did she have to chase down 'bad guys' as Ella had said? There was more to her, too.

Why had she become a cop? Even traffic stops could turn bad.

What does she face on a regular basis?

Breaking the moment, she turned her gaze to the sky.

He licked his lips as his eyes swept the lovely line of her elegant throat, illuminated by the dim back yard lighting and the city's light haze. He resisted the desire to kiss every delicate inch of her exposed skin. He grew hard as his imagination swept lower along her creamy collar bone. Something about her made his body react out of his control. His hands twitched toward her.

He had to be careful. He shoved his hands into his pockets.

So far everything about her was perfect, though she'd seemed hesitant when engaging with him.

He'd told her *no strings attached*, which seemed to be what she wanted, and he'd respect that.

The desire in her eyes when she looked at him pulled him toward her. She clearly wanted him, despite how much he sensed she was holding back.

He wanted her.

He also wanted her to want him back.

Really want him.

He'd been burned too many times in the past. Making the first moves and having it come back to bite him, with the ulterior motives of ambitious women.

He reminded himself that not every woman was like that. He certainly didn't get that vibe from her.

He sensed they were circling this invisible line of uncertainty, which was fair. It had only been a few days since their chance encounter.

Maybe she needed time.

Maybe she knew something about his past? If she did, could she accept him anyway?

Despite his body's insistence, maybe he needed more time too?

The past was the past. It didn't belong in the present, or his future.

She is my future.

He blinked, drawing a breath. His instinct had always guided him. And when he ignored it, things went wrong. When he listened, the world was a glorious place.

Sensing his attention, she turned toward him, reading his expression.

He was still hungry, but not for food.

He was hungry for her smile, for her glance, her company. And most definitely her taste.

His gaze was drawn to her full lips.

Renni had thought of little else since she'd handed him that speeding ticket. And especially since she'd kissed him later that night.

Removing his hands from his pockets, he let them rest at his sides.

Pia placed the ball down on the thick grass, then turned back to him. Her features were set as she reached for his hand and ghosted her fingertips along the outer edge, from wrist to the tip of his little finger.

Renni's pulse leapt into a gallop.

He didn't need a bolder invitation. His fingers curled over hers, pulling her closer to him, then trailed up her bare arm. He watched the goose-flesh rise in the wake of his touch, causing her to shiver.

"Cold?"

She shook her head. The tip of her tongue moistened her lips, eyes trained on his mouth—as his had been on hers.

His hand slid up her nape to bury his fingers in her thick hair as he leaned down to claim her.

Her lips were sweet. Her tongue was delicious as her mouth opened to him.

After a moment, she stepped closer, pressing her breasts to his chest, as her hands roamed his ribs and back.

Renni let her roam, explore, while he concentrated on her mouth, his fingers cradled her lovely face, thumbs gently brushing her cheek bones. After a few more moments when he was done with her mouth, he trailed his lips along her jaw to the delicate flesh just below her ear and inhaled the scent of her warm skin and silky hair. Vanilla and orange.

She shivered again.

His tongue swirled over her flesh, eliciting a gasp.

Her fingers tightened on his sides.

God, he wanted to strip her and admire her under the night sky.

Her body rubbed up against his.

Chest to chest, hip to hip.

There could be no doubt as to his desire for her.

He finally allowed his hands to drift down her body.

Renni reminded himself that he'd told her *no strings*. And he'd meant it. A kiss didn't automatically mean sex. No matter how much he wanted to bury himself in her.

Something about Pia dictated the way he wanted to spend his time with her.

To take his time.

He was surprised when her hands gripped his ass, but pleased all the same.

His instinct whispered there was much to discover about her. That would mean letting her discover more about him too.

That sense of magnetic, arms-length, push-pull circled in him again.

"Should I drive you home, or would you like to stay the night?"

Her eyes rose to his.

There was a long moment as she decided. "I could stay a little while longer," she said.

He looked into her passion-flushed face and swollen mouth. She was the most brilliant of stars, visible, drawing attention, winking through the haze and noise of human life on this planet.

"No strings?" she whispered.

The subtle play of light over her upturned face mesmerized him. He swallowed hard, processing those two words, no longer so sure he could keep his heart in check as he looked into her eyes.

Nor was he prepared to miss an opportunity she was willing to test.

"No strings," he said, resolute, yet deeply conflicted. This was either an incredibly bad idea, or the best thing he'd ever do in his life. And he couldn't put a finger on why that could be.

Her fingers slid over his hands where he held her, then between his own fingers. Linking his hand with hers, she lifted it to her mouth, pressing a kiss to his palm. Raising her gaze to his face, her hand drifted downward, dragging his along her cheek, her throat, and chest to rest on her breast.

He slid his hand further along so that it rested on her ribs, allowing his thumb access to her nipple, and stroked.

Pia's hand slid between their bodies and closed around him, with what sounded like a low growl.

His breath hitched at the unexpected direct contact.

Don't over think this.

As much as he thought he was done with one-night adventures at this point in his life, he would engage in one more.

With Pia.

He had to know if his instinct driving him toward her was right.

He kissed her deeply, tongue swiping hers as he leaned into her heavenly grasp.

SEVEN

Should I drive you home or would you like to stay the night?

Pia studied his face a moment.

Drive me all night...

She blinked as his actual words registered through the building sex haze taking over her brain. Her body was long gone.

"I could stay a little while longer."

His lips on her skin was magical, his tongue erotic.

Renni was so, fucking, hot.

Thick hair and tattoos, with a rocking body.

Sports car *and* motorcycle.

A man that liked to move fast on the road, but so far, with her at least, he'd been moving gentlemanly slow.

A fabulous cook and admirer of stars and mountain getaways, he clearly loved to share his passion of soccer with little kids.

And a perfect gentleman to boot.

Too much perfection. Goddess, did she want him.

She palmed him. Oh, did she *want* him.

She'd thought him arrogant at their first meeting. Not arrogant. Supremely confident. She licked her lips again, rising up on tiptoe to taste the base of his throat at his open collar.

She wanted the satisfaction of hearing the rip as she tore his shirt open, sending buttons flying in all directions. She wanted to lave him *all* over with her tongue.

He seemed to hesitate, despite the shallow rise and fall of his chest.

Like he was waiting for something.

Her fingers opened the first button of his shirt.

"Out here?" She glanced up at him as her mouth found his newly exposed chest. She released another button. Her tongue swirled over his chest bone as his had done below her ear.

"Bedroom?" His voice was tight.

With her hips pressed to his, she could feel him jerk toward her.

She grinned. "I don't care where, Renni. I want you," she whispered, looking into his face.

Decision made, her breath hitched as she looked into his eyes, gauging his reaction to her words.

He glanced up at Ella's balcony.

She whooped in surprise when in the next instant she was swept off her feet. He carried her back into the house with long strides. When he hesitated by the plush couch, she wriggled.

"Here."

"You're sure?" He looked down into her up-turned face, his expression still and serious.

She nodded and he gently returned her to her feet.

"I'm sure."

She turned and pressed him so that he backed up to the couch and sat on the edge, then followed him down.

She knelt between his knees, meeting his mouth as he leaned toward her.

Her fingers fumbled with the next button on his shirt.

Holding her face, his tongue swept hers.

She groaned. Fingers too slow, she rent the shirt open, buttons disappearing into the darkness around them.

Tearing her mouth away, panting, she studied his lean, muscled torso, adorned in intricate ink.

She licked her lips and realized she was purring. Her inner feline was far too close to the surface.

"Pia?"

His concern shook her from her reverie, lost as she was in the sight of his gorgeous body, and stopped purring.

She'd been studying him all evening. Fantasizing about him since before they'd actually met. And here she was, in his living room, and he clearly desired her.

She wanted to fuck him, quick and hard.

She also wanted to savor the experience.

He'd made her dinner, kissed her with utter gentleness, and ensured her consent.

He wasn't in a hurry.

Breathe. Slow down.

Under control, she reached for his hair, carefully untwisting the elastic to let the thick shoulder length curls fall around his face.

Her breath stilled in her chest at his expression. The way he looked at her.

She'd been ready to accept that this was likely a one and done deal. Isn't that what men that lived his lifestyle wanted?

The way he looked at her...it didn't feel like he was a one and done kind of guy.

He wasn't taking what he wanted from her.

He was clearly holding back.

She swallowed. What *did* he want from her?

Keep it simple Pia. Don't read more into this than what you're willing to give.

She was embedded with the local PD and could be transferred out at any time. He was here on contract.

She had a secret. One that, in her experience, most humans didn't react to very well.

How would he react if he found out she was a shifter?

He wouldn't, she decided.

She reached for this belt and unzipped his jeans as she brushed her lips across his, pulling away only long enough to swipe her necklace and blouse up over her head. His large hands were warm on her hips as she unbuttoned her own jeans and pushed them down over her thighs to free her legs, kneeling before him in her lacy bra and panties.

He studied her exposed body for a long moment, then met her eyes with a gentle smile.

"Perfection." His voice was a rasp over her sensitive skin. She shivered.

He pulled her up onto his lap so that she straddled his long, muscular legs. He pressed his lips to the tops of her breasts, his arms encircling her waist.

"You smell like a summer garden," he whispered against the fabric of her bra.

Reaching behind her back, she released the clasps, baring herself to him. The bra dropped to the floor.

His hands slid up to cup her breasts, his thumbs grazed her nipples.

She grew slick as she watched the hunger in his face. She flooded her panties as his tongue glossed over first one nipple, then the other.

Goddess...

Her head fell back, relishing the sensation of his mouth on her.

His hands lifted her up so that he could trail his lips down her midriff to her navel.

Her breath caught when he looked up at her expectantly.

She scrambled off his lap, hooked her fingers under the band of her panties and let them drop.

"You too," she ordered.

He grinned, then stood and slid his jeans and boxers down off his hips. He extracted his wallet from the pocket, withdrew a condom, then let everything else join her little bits of fabric on the floor. The sculpted muscles of his arms, torso, and legs were deeply tanned, darkening the ink that covered much of his arms and part of his chest. Her fingers trailed down the lines of one on his arm, then along the beaded bracelet with a dangling crucifix.

"Are you sure you want this, Pia?" His voice was gruff, pulling her eyes to his face.

Her fingers trailed back up to the inked quote on his arm just below the shoulder.

'You'll never walk alone'.

She swallowed the sudden rise of emotion.

A song fans often sang at the biggest games. Bonds. Companionship. Unity.

Pia stepped close to him, widening her stance just enough so that she stood hip to hip with him, giving him space to slide between her thighs, pressed so intimately to her. He was so hot, his silky flesh scorched her. She desperately wanted him inside her. She was already burning for him, she wanted him to set her ablaze.

How long had it been since she let a man touch her? Probably too long.

No strings.

She wasn't looking for a commitment and she thought he wasn't either.

And she truly wasn't. This felt dangerous.

Need drove her on.

Her hands explored his chest and abs, caressing every ridge of muscle. She resisted the panther-urge to rub her face over every inch of him, claiming him as hers.

Her gaze shot up to his face as he looked at her with hooded eyes.

The urge to claim him was very real.

This was incredibly dangerous. The animalistic need to mate with him was near to overwhelming. Her brain screamed to walk away. Her heart said this could hurt if things went badly.

Her body, prompted by her kitty, was plotting the best positions to enjoy him.

No commitments, she growled at her inner panther, closing her hand around his engorged cock and backing him to the couch.

In a fluid motion, he lowered himself to the thick cushions, taking her with him, so that she straddled him as she had before.

Looking down, she ran her hands up and down his smooth, hard length, feeling his pulse beat in her hands.

Pulling the condom from his grasp, she opened it and discarded the wrapper after extracting the rubber. He helped her unroll it over his length.

Renni's hands slid along her thighs to grip her hips.

She looked up to see his eyes locked on hers. His expression mirrored her own flaming desire. He helped align her to him.

With his tip at her entrance, his fingers gripping her, she slid down with a gasp as he filled her. Her heart pounded as she struggled to control herself.

He closed his eyes and leaned his head back on the couch cushions. His throat worked as he swallowed and his chest rose in deep breaths, fingers still clutching her hips as she rested, encasing him within her.

She leaned forward, eliciting a groan from deep in his chest. Pressing her lips to his exposed throat she inhaled deeply of his scent.

Each time, committing him deeper and deeper to her primal memory.

She reveled in the intimacy of the sensation of him pulsing deep inside of her.

He lifted his head, leveling her with his dark gaze, holding her.

A moment longer, she studied him.

No longer Renni Diaz the soccer superstar.

He was Renni, the man who enjoyed fast cars and motorbikes, loved to cook, loved to share his passion of sports with children and—she was about to learn—was a slow, deliberate lover.

He held her gaze as they became attuned to one another's expressions and vulnerabilities.

He remained motionless until she tilted her hips back again to begin the writhe—the dance of passion on his lap. And he met her, matching her rhythm, adding force and need, grinding and thrusting, forcing gasps and cries to escape her every time he slammed that magical spot at the inner end of her channel, until it was too much.

Much too much, and she landed somewhere in the galaxy, surrounded by light and color and the sensation of Renni holding her close. A sensation that called to some deeply buried part of her. The part that stopped her from tying herself to anyone that came into her life.

A GENTLE BREEZE FLUTTERED over Pia's leg, prompting her to open her eyes. The sweet sounds of crickets and frogs drifting in through the window hinted she wasn't at home. Renni's unique masculine scent and the scents of their lovemaking enveloped her.

Oh yes.

At some point, they'd climbed the stairs to his bedroom.

After their initial romp on the couch, Renni had really slowed things down.

Savored her.

Explored every part of her body.

Always making love to her, eye to eye.

She'd never experienced anything so erotic

Pia had never, ever, felt so worshiped.

She extracted herself from the sheets twined around her limbs, carefully, so as not to disturb him. She watched the steady rise and fall of his chest in sleep, her eyes drawn up to his face.

He was a beautiful man.

She hesitated in her extraction for a moment to allow herself to really look at him, now that he wouldn't see. His dark hair curled in a wild cloud around his head on the pillow. The tension around his brows and mouth was relaxed, allowing her to see the truer angle of each. The moonlight made his sun-kissed skin richer. His jaw line was accentuated by the new growth of facial hair, which drew more attention to his soft lips.

She wanted to spend all her time exploring those lips. Lips that made her sigh. Lips that made her moan.

She quickly ejected the memory and focused on her mission, before she reached for him again: To leave without waking him.

She needed to get home. She needed to re-orient herself before work. Slip back into her routine.

This—her eyes swept Renni again—was a fantasy whose wispy tendrils of fairy tale longing had begun to caress her heart. She needed distance and clarity.

She needed to run.

The sheets whispered traitorously as she slid from the bed. She glanced back as Renni stirred but didn't wake. As soon as he settled and the even rise and fall of his breathing resumed, she padded out of the room and collected her clothing from around the living room where they'd been discarded.

Stuffing everything, including her boots, into her over-sized bag she looked around, feeling like she was forgetting something.

She huffed, unable to recall what she might be missing and glanced out the window. She had to go before the sky lightened too much. With practiced silence, she moved out onto the terrace, bag in hand, letting herself out of the yard through the latched gate.

With a quick glance to ensure no one observed her from a nearby yard or window, she shifted.

The magic shimmered around her as her hands and feet thinned and elongated into paws. Fur prickled below the surface of her skin as it erupted. Her soft human body turned into that of a sleek, muscled panther.

Her ears twitched, listening. Her nose sought the scents of the neighborhood. As far as she could tell, all were asleep.

Time to go.

She looped her head through the handles of her bag, ignoring the sense of how ridiculous she looked.

It was so worth it.

An amazing night with Renni. So sweet, so generous, so frikking hot.

If she wasn't careful, she could want more.

I do want more.

She grunted the thought away and focused on her route home.

Keep it simple.

Memories of their lovemaking chased her home.

Making her way through obscured places, she picked up scents of other animals and the distinct tang of shifters now and then, as she went.

As soon as she was close to her apartment, she crept to one of her 'safe' spots and resumed her human shape, dressed, and walked the last two blocks. Home, she immediately went into the shower. As she lathered her hypersensitive flesh, her mind was pulled back to him again and again. The feel of his warm skin on hers, his lips and teeth... those hands.

She slid her fingers into herself and over her nub in an effort to relieve the rekindled sexual desire.

Somewhat sated, she dried off and slid between the cool sheets of her bed to sleep a few more hours before she had to get ready for work.

EIGHT

RENNI PULLED THE HEAVY door to the police station open and stepped inside, then walked up to the counter.

He'd taken a guess that Pia's shift would end about now and asked the clerk for her. As soon as the clerk picked up the desk phone to make the call, his fingers drummed the countertop and he turned away to mitigate the rising anxiety, shoving his hands into his pockets.

His thumb slid over the hard sphere in his pocket again and again. It anchored the memory—the reality of the previous night. She'd left him in the night, leaving only traces of her presence. The dishes, the wild tangle of his bed sheets and the lingering scent of their lovemaking in his bedroom. And her necklace, which he'd found under the coffee table in the living room.

He cleared his throat, redirecting his thoughts, else he'd end up with another hard on. His new state of being every time he thought of Pia now, all throughout the day.

Returning her necklace was the polite thing to do, no matter that he knew it was really an excuse to see her again.

Last night hadn't been enough.

Another day of training and meetings. More pressure for him to lead the gala. Sophy had suggested they could attend together, since he didn't have anyone in town. He'd turned her down as politely as possible, unable to avoid the obvious sting of rejection, and said he actually did have someone.

He just hoped Pia would help him not make a liar of himself.

She'd slipped away without a word. Maybe she didn't want to see him again.

He drew a deep breath, realizing his heart was pounding the way it did when he was lining up a penalty shot. And in the same way he handled stress on the pitch, he drew a deep breath and centered himself. He'd make the punt. He'd face victory or defeat after the ball landed where it would. Once the choices were airborne, it would be up to her.

"Renni?"

He spun at her voice and smiled.

The surprise was evident in her expression as she approached him. He didn't let his smile falter when she didn't return it.

She looked sexy as all hell. She stood in a straight-backed, authoritative stance, with her hair pulled into a braid. She wore her uniform with ease.

They moved out of earshot of the clerk, and no one else occupied the public space.

"I was on my way home and wanted to return this to you." He held out the pendant and chain he pulled from his pocket, feeling like a thirteen-year-old boy again.

She smiled then, reaching for it. "Thank you, Renni." She looked at him, smile widening. "You didn't have to do that. I could have retrieved it the next time we went for a drink." Her lips tilted with a hint of mischief.

"I had a favor to ask, too."

While she maintained her smile, her eyes glimmered with suspicion. "Okay."

"Would you attend a charity gala with me?"

Her brows shot up and she dropped her gaze to the golden soccer ball in her hand. "Wow. Uhm..."

He pulled the card from his pocket that he'd already written the details on. "Think about it and call me."

Pia took the card from his fingers, reading it. She drew a deep breath, staring at the card, then snapped the edge of it against the fingers of the closed hand that held the gold necklace. Finally, she said, "I guess I'll have to go shopping."

Renni's heart hammered as though his penalty kick had just soared flawlessly past defenders and keeper, swooshing right into the back of the net.

He grinned. "When do we go?"

She laughed. "You want to shop with me? I'm a terrible shopper."

"Absolutely." He stepped closer, forcing her to tilt her gaze higher. Jesus, her lips were delicious. He lowered his face to hers. He didn't miss the slight catch in her breath as his fingers swept her jaw. "I can't get enough of you," he whispered.

She drew a quick breath. "Last night I-"

"Last night was perfect." He lowered his lips to hers, savoring her response.

There was no doubt she still wanted him.

Someone cleared their throat.

Renni released Pia's lips and looked up to see a stern, older, uniformed man.

She turned toward the newcomer.

"Constable Jensen, you're needed."

"Yes, Captain," she said to him, then turned her attention back to Renni. "I'm done in an hour."

"Meet you at the pub?"

She grinned. "You got it."

Pia followed Captain Bergeron to his office, closing the door behind her.

"I just read your report. You're sure there's a paranormal involved in Hare and Maliki's case?" He sat behind his desk.

She nodded. "As I said in our call with agent Cole, yes. Despite the scant traces, I'm sure. I haven't been able to pinpoint who or what kind specifically yet. I went back to have another look. Just some sort of unfamiliar shifter. They're careful. I'm going to follow up in the community and see what else I can find out."

The older man stared hard at her, brow furrowed, processing. "Huh."

Since she'd arrived, she'd helped close out several small cases, deeming them perpetrated by paranormals. The information was being passed up the bureaucratic levels to whoever needed to know in the Canadian government, so they could decide what to do with them. All Pia knew was that she was to report to the captain and her GPSA team leader.

"The thieves that were arrested didn't know much, so this shifter could be the one heading everything. The one with contacts that gets the goods out into the black market. He may just find a new crew."

The captain nodded. "I'll talk to Hare and Maliki and see if they have any new leads."

Pia turned to go.

"Renni Diaz, huh?"

Hand on the doorknob, she turned back to the Captain.

"Good soccer player."

She smiled, waiting to see where he was going with this.

"High profile, gonna make it hard for you to stay low key."

"He just invited me to a charity gala."

The Captain let out a whistle. "The media is going to run with that."

"I know." She had considered the risks of interacting with Renni on a public scale.

International soccer superstar dating local cop.

She had a strong cover. She'd let that be her protection against her true identity.

"Your team leader is aware?"

Pia stiffened.

"And when Mr. Diaz finds out you're a shifter?"

"I'll handle it *if* it ever comes up. Are we done here, sir?"

"Just keep in mind that whatever you do, it reflects on this department."

"My personal life doesn't belong to the department."

"When you step into the sphere of a man like that, there is no longer a 'personal' life."

She shrugged. "Maybe this will be good for the department. Raise its profile with the public."

He rose from his seat, countering. "Or question our integrity."

She stiffened. "Do not pin the reputation of this precinct on me. There are plenty of other people here you should be scrutinizing."

"None of them are throwing themselves in front of the media. If you were one of my own-"

"Which I'm not."

"—I'd advise you to reconsider."

"Would you? If I were male, I seriously doubt you'd say anything to me at all."

The captain straightened and opened his mouth to speak. Pia cut him off.

"I haven't been here for years and years, but long enough to see the inequities and behaviors. Maybe you should take your blinders off if you want to scrutinize anyone, take a hard look at a few of your 'own' and let me do what I came here to do. And stay out of my personal business."

Silent, he seemed to consider her words.

The agreement between the GPSA and local PD was for a one-year trial. She only had a couple of months left before she'd be reassigned. She was always, *always*, going to be an outsider. Except maybe within her own squad. That was the one place she'd finally felt a sense of belonging.

The captain had been ordered to accept her placement. And he had, grudgingly. He didn't know her well. Not only was she not a local, she also wasn't even a Canadian—or a human. Too many factors.

"I know you'll be there to represent the precinct, as will some other captains and officers from across the city. I'd be just another face for the city department along with all the others."

She was tired of being expected to prove herself. It was part of the job, unfortunately.

"Is that all?"

He gave her a sharp nod, brows furrowed impossibly further.

NINE

RENNI GLANCED UP WITH a smile as a figure approached his table at the *Chatton Noir*.

He stood, smile faltering on seeing Pia's dark expression. "What's wrong?"

He'd meant to kiss her when she arrived. Instead, he gestured toward the empty chair across from him, maintaining his distance.

She offered a half-hearted smile and blew out her breath. "Work conflicts. No need to worry."

"Is it a problem that I showed up at the precinct?"

She considered him a long moment before answering. "Honestly, yes, I guess so. But so is me being seen here with you."

His heart lurched and the muscles in his shoulders tightened.

She bit her lip, as though she was chewing on her thoughts before saying them. "The captain is old school and has concerns about one of his female officers being associated with someone like you—with a high profile and-"

"A reputation?" He retrieved his seat after she settled on hers. He picked up his soda water and sipped, considering what to say next.

She still wore her uniform. None of the ease she'd shown around him the night before was evident.

He continued. "I haven't been in that party world for years and yet, reputations, once gained, are hard to shake. You've changed your mind about the gala."

Her dark eyes shimmered in the low light and he thought he caught a glimpse of something...else, in them. She blinked and it was gone.

"It's alright, Pia. From the start we agreed there were no obligations between us. Perhaps last night was a mistake."

"No." She drew in a quick breath. When she spoke again her voice was soft but firm. "Last night was not a mistake—at least, not for me."

Her hand appeared over the table. She pressed her palm down on the surface.

He could feel the unasked question in her tone and expression.

"No. No, it wasn't for me either."

"It's just...complicated."

Renni nodded. He'd seen it time and gain among his teammates. It was easier to be the playboy, partying, going from woman to woman. The media soaked it up. Expected it. When the thrill of the fast pace wore thin, and the media beast began to starve, things got complicated. It still wanted—expected to be fed and would scavenge for any scrap it could.

So far, here in Montreal, things had been quiet. There were fans that approached him, and he'd gladly given them his time. He'd begun to relax.

The media focus had mostly moved on, now that he was out of the European sphere of that lifestyle.

This gala was a global event. Eyes would be back on him. And on Pia if they attended together. The media would no doubt turn its attention to her. Would it blow over quickly?

Her hand rubbed across the rough surface of the table, her middle finger following a scar. Then another. "I like you, Renni. A lot."

Ah, here it is. He couldn't stop his entire body from going rigid.

But.

It had been a long, long time since he'd been dumped. So long that he'd forgotten what it felt like.

His gut churned as he processed his emotions.

Like a perfect goal, ruled offline.

A glorious run, eyes set, nimble dodges of attacking defenders and the punt striking the back of the net. The shrill whistle halting everything, cutting off the feeling of glory.

The glaring orange flag signaling the end.

Pia's eyes remained down cast, fixated on the table.

"I like you too, Pia. I suppose this is where we either continue on as friends or part ways."

Her gaze shot to his face. She licked her lips, her head dipped in a nod that didn't seem convincing. She bit her lip again, hesitating before speaking. "I'll be leaving Montreal in a couple of months. I'm scheduled to transfer out. I only planned to be here for my dad then move on."

She'd mentioned her father before.

His gut told him there was more she wasn't telling him. Was it normal for a police officer to only serve one year in a region? Not that he knew much about how it all worked. He could see how the need to be close to her ill father might be a special circumstance.

"You'll return home? You said you were from upstate New York? That's not so far." He said, trying to keep the sound of hope out of his tone. In the beginning he'd said *no strings*, the truth was he wanted to bind her to him with all the rope and chain he could find. That's what his heart told him—and that surprised the hell out of him.

He swallowed that realization with another sip of his drink before setting it back onto the table between them.

Her head shook. "No, I don't think so. I don't know where I'll be sent next."

Sent?

She stood. "Unless you've reconsidered, I'm still willing to attend with you."

"No." Instinct prompted the quick response. He smiled to ease the tension that had built between them. "Shopping excursion tomorrow?"

Her expression turned dubious. "I'm a terrible shopper, Renni."

"So, you said before." He shrugged. "I'm hoping this will give me more time to discover some of your secrets." He grinned.

Her body jerked upright. "What makes you think I have secrets?"

Surprised by her defensive reaction, he said, "every woman has secrets."

Every man too.

He shoved the thought aside. "Ten o'clock?"

Her keen eyes studied his face a few seconds longer, then nodded. "I'll meet you at Notre Dame Square."

PIA WENT HOME, SHOWERED, and dressed in jeans and a plain shirt; heart hammering all the while.

Her hands trembled as she ran the brush through her wet hair, staring at herself in the fogged bathroom mirror.

Her panther had nearly taken over during that brief conversation with Renni, when he'd jumped to the conclusion that she'd changed her mind about the gala. He was offering her an 'out', which her panther had firmly refused.

None of this was really about the captain's judgment.

It had just been a prompt to force her to consider what was really happening here.

She'd convinced herself that she was just stroking her curiosity about a man whose career she'd followed for years. Dabbling in some fun with a gorgeous guy. Enjoying the attention of a wanted superstar.

Of course, it was expected that he'd been a playboy in his younger years.

The reality was, she was coming to see that he wasn't anymore—If he ever had been, truly.

The undertones of this relationship felt much, much deeper.

Dangerous.

Those wispy fairy tale tendrils returned, wrapping around both of them, trying to finish a spell they'd both begun.

She tried to separate her kitty's instinctual drive, shoving her toward Renni, from what Pia actually wanted. The problem was kitty always won out in the end. No matter how much Pia resisted.

Renni had hooked her with the thrill of the motorcycle ride, then reeled her in with an incredibly satisfying home-cooked dinner and netted her with amazing sex.

No. Not just sex.

She didn't dare *want* him.

A human.

A human with the eyes of the world on him.

Pia was an undercover paranormal agent. A shifter. She didn't belong in the light of the world's eyes. She was meant to prowl in the darkest of shadows.

She drew a shaky breath.

Which is where she meant to go now. There was work to do.

Pia ascended from the subway access to the humid, crowded party district. Her sensitive hearing was overwhelmed by the sounds of conversation punctuated by laughter and blaring car horns as she moved along St. Catherine's Street toward her target. With a quick glance to ensure there weren't any eyes on her, she ducked down an inky alley. Music thumped through the brick wall, filling the narrow space. Another glance toward the mouth of the alley and she slipped around the corner to the back of the building and descended the crumbling concrete steps to the handless steel door and turned her face to the security camera as she pushed the button affixed to the thick frame.

Seconds later the door clicked and released enough to slide her fingers around the edge and open it. Once inside, she pulled it closed and made her way through the interior door where she met her host.

She grinned.

Erin.

Startling blue eyes glimmered at her from a round freckled face and unruly cloud of curly brown hair.

She was even shorter than Pia. As she approached, Erin threw her arms around her and gave her a full, welcoming kiss on her lips. For a moment, Pia gave in to the familiar comfort and returned Erin's kiss.

Eyes closed, she sighed.

Erin's embrace loosened.

When Pia reopened her eyes, Erin's were locked on her face.

"What's changed?" Erin asked.

Pia reached up, fingers brushing an errant curl back from Erin's forehead.

"You've met someone." Erin said.

Pia smiled. "You never miss a thing."

Disappointment skittered across Erin's lovely features. She found her smile for Pia. "I guess this means no more romps? It's serious? This feels serious." She let her arms fall away.

"My panther has set her sights on someone and is not giving me much choice."

"Ah. A mate."

Pia cringed. "Would seem so. I can't see how it's going to work, though. It can't."

Erin lifted a brow. "Sounds mysterious. Come and have a drink and we can talk *all* about her? Him?" Erin's hands slid down Pia's arms to her fingers, lingering in the spaces between, unable to let her go just yet.

"Him. Sure, but that's not why I'm here."

"Business first, then. Boy talk later," she said, pulling Pia along toward her office. "That doesn't stop you from telling me who he is along the way."

Pia glanced down at the naked curiosity in Erin's face as she grinned up at her.

"Renni Diaz," she said, quick and matter of fact.

Erin stumbled. "Fuck. Me." Her round eyes searched Pia's face. "You're not kidding."

Pia shook her head.

"Well, assuming he isn't a paranormal, that complicates the shit out of things, doesn't it?"

Shrugging, Pia said, "he's human. If he's a human with abilities, I couldn't say, but I don't think so."

Erin seemed to consider this. Then broke into a mischievous grin. "Look at you bagging one of the hottest athletes in the world. Is the sex amazing? I bet it's amazing with a guy like that."

"Business first."

"You'll give me the details after, right?"

Pia lifted a shoulder as she moved through the doorway into Erin's cramped office. Out of habit, she glanced at the secondary door that led to Erin's personal space. She didn't think Renni was into open relationships. And somehow, she didn't think her panther was going to let her carry on with anyone other than Renni at this point. She sighed. She was going to miss that special intimacy she shared with Erin.

"We both knew it was temporary, Pia," Erin said, studying her face.

"Are you sure you're not psychic?"

Erin laughed. "You're just terrible at hiding your feelings. At least from me." She poured whiskey into two tumblers, handing one to Pia.

"We've just known each other too long."

"Business," Erin said, settling into her chair, propping her feet on her desk with a cursory glance at the monitors above it.

Pia claimed the other, eyes sweeping the screens too. "Unusual shifters in the area. Unfamiliar scent. Not a species I'm familiar with."

Erin nodded, pursing her lips, considering. She blew out a breath, turning her attention back to the monitors as she thought.

The first monitor's camera was pointed at the back door where Pia had come in. Several other screens held images of empty hallways. The others were alive with activity. Two more pointed at the street-side entrance where a loose crowd formed a line beside Max and Ray, Erin's bouncers. The rest surveyed the club space—dance floor, the bar where Dave worked, tables, VIP spaces, washroom access points, and staff spaces.

Pia suppressed the rising desire to go and lose herself on the dance floor amid a writhing sea of strangers. Most of the club sounds were muffled in the private, insulated space of Erin's office, but a few beats drifted in.

"Unusual species," Erin whispered, searching the screens. "You're going to give me details, right?" she murmured, eyes locked on one in particular.

"Erin, you know I don't kiss and tell. Who are you looking at?"

"Is he better than me?"

Pia turned her attention to her oldest and dearest friend's face. Pia hadn't expected the raw vulnerability in Erin's expression.

"No matter how much we agree there are no expectations between us, it's hard to ignore what the heart wants."

Pia swallowed hard. "Erin, no one will ever be better than you," she whispered, cradling her lover's face between her palms.

Erin nodded, blinking quickly, not looking at Pia directly. "I love you, too. Now enough of this nonsense. No more friends with benefits." She sniffed and pulled away from Pia's hands. "These two," she said, pointing at two guys seated in one of the VIP rooms, clearly in a meeting with several others. "Your timing is wicked. These two have been coming around for some time now, and every now and then rent the room for meetings. The guys they meet with look serious."

Pia knew Erin wouldn't say much more than that on the matter. She walked a fine line between Pia's world and the underworld that couldn't be tipped. Not if she wanted to stay in business.

"Unusual shifters? What are they?"

Erin nodded. "Hyena."

Pia straightened, watching the black and white screen. Not much was happening as they talked.

She'd never met hyena shifters before.

A fair-haired woman crossed into view to stand next to the men, her back to the camera. "Who is this?"

"Not sure. She only ever attends the meetings. I don't usually see her in the club space."

"Thanks."

Erin grabbed her hand before she could leave. "Pia, I know how much relationships terrify you. You need to learn to trust. Trust your kitty. Trust yourself. I wish you happiness."

Pia stared at their linked fingers as she considered how to voice what was in her heart. "It's because of you that I've learned to trust my squad. And I'm learning to trust myself."

Erin stood, still holding Pia's hand. She leaned forward, brushing her lips across Pia's. "I know."

Pia pressed her forehead to Erin's.

As Erin finally pulled away, she grinned. "Pizza next Thursday?"

"Absolutely."

TEN

WHEN PIA CROSSED NOTRE Dame square, she spotted Renni sitting on the wide stone steps to the cathedral. She glanced at the time on her phone before tucking it into her pocket. It was still ten before the hour.

"You're early. Have you been waiting long?"

He stood with a smile when he saw her. "Not at all. I just came out," he said, nodding toward the church doors.

She eyed him, curious. "You practice?"

Renni shrugged. "Now and then. Old habits. I went in to light candles for my mother and father." His fingers seemed to unconsciously drift over the looped rosary of his opposite wrist as he looked at the building. Turning his attention back to Pia he said, "shall we get started on this great shopping expedition?"

"I'm warning you, I'm very picky."

"As am I. Shows you have taste." He winked at her, taking up her hand as she led him away from the church.

Later, after unsuccessful visits to several stores, Pia and Renni wandered along old Montreal's cobblestoned streets, ice cream cones in hand in an attempt to cool off in the hot weather.

They laughed often, trying to save the cones from dripping while also avoiding tourists along the narrow sidewalks. A competition of who could keep their cones from dripping ensued as the drips picked up speed and volume.

Renni won by shoving most of the cone in his mouth, resulting in a brain freeze that had Pia doubled over in laughter, allowing the top half of her ice cream to drop with a splat on the stone promenade.

Every once in a while, one of those tourists would gape as they passed, then a moment later come running back asking for a selfie with Renni, who always obliged with a friendly smile. Pia managed to keep herself out of the way by offering to take the pictures for the fan.

They wandered back toward Notre Dame and Place d'Armes square, where a gang of kids played while their parents rested on nearby benches. The children rushed over on seeing Renni while he and Pia paused to study the stone work of the Chomedey monument and fountain. The kids' excitement on seeing Renni was highly animated as they offered whatever they could find for him to sign. Their parents stood in a group looking on happily. The noise of their excitement followed them down the narrow street as they disappeared.

"You're pretty good at that." Pia commented once they'd gone.

Renni looked up from the rippling fountain water and smiled. "Fans come first. They are the reason any club exists. No matter what the managers and owners think." He shrugged. "I'm sure it's the same for your job. The public comes first, right?"

Pia nodded. She considered her own job.

"Does it ever get taxing?"

"On occasion someone gets a little... too involved. Some a little over excited. Most people are respectful."

They stepped up to the corner, waiting for the streetlight to change so they could cross.

Pia led the way to the nearest metro entrance making their way down and across town via Montreal's underground city. They re-emerged above ground, walking until they found the dress shop Renni had found online for Pia in the heart of the city's couture district. Not having found anything suitable through the entire morning, Renni had done a search on his phone while Pia bought the cones.

Preceding him through the door, her gut knotted, her whole body tensed. She didn't have to graze the tags to know this was going to be a big purchase. Maybe she could find something that could be worn to another event...if she ever went to another event.

This just wasn't her thing. She was an agent.

Maybe the captain was right.

This was a bad, bad idea.

She glanced at Renni, who studied her, with a grin.

"Anything you want," he whispered.

"I'll pay for it myself," she said, eying him with suspicion.

His grin spread as he leaned toward her, lips close to her ear. "If I pay for it, I won't feel guilty if I decide to rip it off you." His fingers swept up her inner wrist.

A shiver rippled through her.

"What makes you think I'd want that?"

"I know some of your secrets now." He challenged, the gleam in his eyes when he looked at her made her mouth dry.

Images of their night together rolled through her mind. She licked her lips. He wasn't wrong. Then she remembered. "Sorry about your shirt."

"Don't be."

"A dress with buttons on the back?" She offered, deciding she liked the idea of him wanting to rip her clothes off of her.

He nodded. "Perfect."

Pia had never let anyone dress her before—never thought she ever would. She bit her lip as he moved away, giving her space to browse. After a few moments a clerk approached her. An hour later, she'd made her choice, her measurements had been taken for alteration, and a pickup time arranged.

Renni was settling the bill while Pia inspected a few of the accessories on a display by the door as it opened, emitting a gust of unfamiliar-shifter-laced wind.

Pia glanced up to see a striking blonde enter the shop. The woman ignored Pia's presence as she bypassed her, despite the twitch of her nose belying the acknowledgment of her scent.

"Renni! What brings you in here, of all places?" The woman stood blocking the aisle.

"Shopping for your gala with my date," he said, looking across the clothing displays to Pia.

Pia approached.

The back of the woman resembled that of the woman Pia had seen in Erin's security monitor of the VIP room at the club. Pia moved in beside Renni with a smile.

Renni introduced her to his co-worker, "This is Sophy Khienak. She organized the charity event preceding the gala for the club."

"Sounds like you've done a lot of work, I look forward to the evening," Pia said, noting the unusual tightness in Renni's voice.

Sophy's smile was anything but friendly, though it was meant to be. "Renni's never mentioned a significant other before. What a lovely surprise."

Pia's inner panther growled at the baring of teeth in her false smile. The woman's tangy scent permeated the space under the mask of her perfume. Not wolf, coyote, or cat. Familiar in some way, but not recognizable.

"The dresses are lovely here; I hope you find what you're looking for." Pia reached for Renni's hand, laced her fingers through his. "I'm starving, let's grab dinner." After a breath, she said, "Would you like to join us?"

Sophy's eyes lingered on their linked hands, her smile widening so that Pia thought her face would crack. "Thank you, no. I have shopping to do. You love birds enjoy yourselves." She flipped a long curl over her shoulder. "I'll see you at work, Renni," she called after them.

Neither said a word for about half a block, before Pia stopped in front of a tiny bubble tea shop. "Thirsty? We can get drinks while we decide where to eat."

Renni opened the door for her. They ordered sugarless milk tea and taro drinks and stepped aside to wait for the order.

"So." Pia began. "She's... nice."

Renni huffed. "Yes. Nice."

Pia's brow rose. He didn't elaborate.

"Thanks for agreeing to go."

She grinned. "I'm really only in it for the shredding of the dress event at this point. I was kind of on the fence before. Now I'm all in."

He laughed, and the sound rippled through her.

SOPHY SAT IN HER car, staring at Renni Diaz's house from partway down the street. She'd been sitting in her car since the streetlights came on, waiting for the sky to fully darken.

She hadn't been able to shake the incident at the dress shop; running into Renni and his date. The moment replayed over and over in her mind.

A shifter.

Must be recent.

He'd told her he had a date for the Gala, but Sophy hadn't scented another woman on Renni before, let alone a shifter.

Did he know?

If he didn't, how would he react?

Sophy bit her lip. She needed to know more.

Was he home yet, or would he be spending the night with her?

She ground her teeth and got out of her car, easing the door closed with a soft click, to avoid unwanted attention. Dressed in a plain flowing tunic and light flats in case she had to unexpectedly shift, she slipped into the shadows and wove her way around the side of Renni's house. She pulled a pair of latex gloves from her pocket and put them on. Having been here before, months ago, she knew there was a gate at the side and let herself into the back yard that way before making her way to the patio door. On seeing all the lights off, she pulled a three-inch, slim handled screwdriver from the deep pocket of her loose dress, then jimmied the door, bypassing the lock with very little noise. Easing the door open, she stepped inside, listening.

The house was empty.

Her sensitive nose twitched, scenting, walking further into the house. The woman's feline scent was present. Faint. Lingering. Not recent. Not living here.

She relaxed her shoulders moving closer to the items displayed on the shelves.

Maybe she could still win Renni over. Help him see that they would be perfect together. She'd already tried once, and he'd politely, professionally, turned her down. Yes, she'd been angry that he hadn't understood her work to make him the center of the gala was to help spotlight him. She could help raise his star even higher.

That would drive Lucas insane.

Or maybe she'd just enjoy both of them. Fantasies of both men pleasuring her at once rolled through her, stealing her breath, making her slick and throbbing.

Lucas would never go for that.

Or would he? The hate-fucking would be amazing.

Unless Renni believed he was well above her; her efforts meaningless. Worthless.

And there was this other woman now. Pia something or other. Other than the fact that she was a shifter, there was nothing remarkable about her. Plain.

Sophy's back straightened.

Her feet were light on the stairs as she went up, then in and out of the upper rooms, casing. Renni's agent had said he didn't have anything left to auction—if he wasn't lying—maybe there was something else of value.

Doubt wormed its way to the forefront of her mind.

She stepped into a room set up like an office and approached the desk. The file drawer was locked. Pulling her screwdriver from her pocket again, she slipped the lock and eased it open, walking her fingers over the folder tabs. Bills, car maintenance, family, finance.

The bills were mundane household expenses, as were the car records. The finance folder was empty. She blew out her breath. On-line banking, no doubt. Welcome to the paperless world.

Family. Old letters from his father. A quick perusal indicated a strained relationship. Apologies for all of the terrible trouble, pleas to understand, pride in his career. Wasn't his father dead? She scanned through them, then shoved them back into the drawer. "Useless."

She'd give him another chance to accept her help. Otherwise... fuck him. She wouldn't waste her time and efforts on someone that couldn't see how much she had to offer.

A thrill rippled through her.

Either she'd have him, or she'd bury him.

Lucas could do whatever the fuck he wanted with Renni.

Sophy wasn't going to let any man treat her like she was sub-par. She didn't care who he was.

Lucas popped into her mind again. He was an exception. That man knew how to make her beg.

She went into the last room, stopping next to the bed. It smelled only of Renni. Like the rest of the house, the furnishings and personal touches were minimal. He was here on contract, not enough time to make it a home.

Unless she could get him to want to stay with the club, with her.

Her eyes lingered on the neat, rumple-free duvet and carefully straightened pillows. Her fingers stretched toward the nearest pillow and pulled it to her face. Inhaling deeply of his scent in the darkness of his room, her panties dampened. Well-developed fantasies flickered through her mind, imagining her body entwined with his, or her fingers gripping the headboard as he pounded into her from behind. She groaned, quivering, hands crushing the pillow to her face, resisting the urge to slip her fingers into herself.

She froze as the sound of an engine approached, then let out her breath as it continued on past the house and disappeared again.

She replaced the pillow and drew a deep breath regaining her self-control.

Glancing toward the walk-in closet, she turned her body and focus back to her purpose. Nestled on the floor was a heavy personal fireproof safe, like most of the other houses in this neighborhood. She hadn't seen the code among the files. It was a solid enough dial safe, but she was skilled.

She settled on the floor, pressing her ear to the door, her fingers light on the dial.

Sophy had found two of the numbers when she heard another car approaching. This time the engine geared down as it turned into a driveway. A second later, the thunk and rumble of the house's garage door sounded, alerting her to Renni's return.

She was down the stairs and easing out of the patio door before he reached the inner door from the garage to the house. The kitchen light flicked to life as she stepped into the shadow next to the door, listening as he moved through the room, dropping items onto the countertop. With her keen sense of hearing, every one of his movements was loud and crisp inside the house. His shadow filled the splash of light on the terrace, and she held her breath, sliding away, her back to the house as she watched the dark image.

Moments later she was back in her car.

Starting the engine, she breathed a sigh of relief, eased the car forward with darkened lights until she reached the stop sign. Flicking them on, she signaled left, and drove home to process what she'd seen. If any of it could be of use or was a total waste of time.

Not a complete waste of time.

She shivered at the memory of moving, unin-vited, unseen through his home. His sanctuary.

His most private domain.

ELEVEN

PIA LET RENNI DROP her off at her apartment building. He got out of the car to walk her to the door and let her go with a lingering kiss that almost had her dragging him by the collar all the way up to her bed. Almost.

She kicked off her jeans and replaced her blouse with an over-sized tee shirt before settling at her kitchen table.

Determined to turn her thoughts to other things, she pulled the robbery files from her drawer and went over them along with her notes and map of the city again. There were other cases to be worked on as well. Something about this one pulled her attention first.

The robberies were all in the more affluent areas. A number of them in Renni's neighborhood, and a couple scattered elsewhere. Wealthy, obviously. Was there anything else in common? Businessmen and women, socially active in the community, collectors.

Two of the thieves had been caught and were keeping their mouths shut tight. Hare and Maliki had felt there was someone else involved. Cop instinct. Pia was inclined to agree. She'd suspected a shifter, but the scenes she'd visited weren't recent enough for her to get a good lock on potential scent signatures. She'd picked up the cases too late in the game. She couldn't be all places and doing all things at once. Still, she was here to do what she could.

What the city's force really needed was their own division. Or Cole and Bergeron needed to find someone more permanent than herself.

Pia quickly brushed aside memories of her father in the last months of his illness, before he let go. She drew a shaky breath and turned her attention back to the file.

Focus: A concept that had been impossible for months after she lost him, but was slowly coming back. She picked up the printouts of the articles preceding and following the robberies. Charity events that the victims were involved in. Coincidences or threads?

She was reminded of the gala Renni had invited her to and the run of shopping they'd done that day. She smiled. He was an easy guy to be around. It hadn't taken her long to process her fan-girl inclination and set it aside like an adult woman, even though she'd been watching Renni's career for years. Soccer was the thing she'd shared with her dad, even when they were apart, they'd try to 'talk' while watching the games from their own places. Texting, video or voice calls, sharing the moments. And her dad had been a big fan of Renni's previous club. Renni had an impressive career, playing for all the top clubs, right back into his early training grounds. She vaguely recalled the tabloid and the trouble that seemed to follow him wherever he went. Despite his successful career, he couldn't seem to shake personal turmoil that went public.

She recalled what the captain had said about stepping into the public sphere. They were involved, yet not invested—so long as she was careful. She nodded as though convincing herself. His charisma was a strong, strong magnet that was difficult to resist. Filaments of her being stretched toward him, slowly weaving into threads.

Especially when he smiled. It seemed to come easy, genuine.

A gentleman with a kind heart. A noble heart.

And then there was her panther. Pia's logical mind denied belief in fated mates. She'd struggled against it when her mother had died far too young, and her father had faded.

A shifter and a human.

Just like herself and Renni.

The bond had been there, and her father had suffered the loss for such a long time. Pia's mother's people had spurned their little family because of her father's humanity. And her own. They weren't welcome. They'd only ever had each other.

And over the years, anyone that had found out her secrets—whether it was another shifter discovering her human half, or a human discovering her shifter self—she'd been rejected.

Except for Erin, the only other being she'd ever met that knew what it was to be an outsider on so many levels.

Pia couldn't avoid a pang of guilt at the feeling of betraying her dearest friend. They'd never been exclusive or committed to each other—or anyone else.

They both understood when the beast made a decision, nothing could supersede it.

Pia just never dreamed it would ever apply to herself.

She sighed and reached for her discarded laptop and dragged it across the table toward herself, booting it up. Renni's beautiful smile shone in her mind. She smiled back.

Genuine. Not like the frozen mannequin smile his colleague had presented that day.

Shifter. Unfamiliar shifter.

Could she—?

No. But...?

Pia closed her eyes to dissect the thoughts and analyze the impulse. Gut instinct or jealously? What had Renni said her name was? Sonya? Sophia? No—Sophy.

Reaching for a pen, she found there were none on the table with her stuff. Rising from the chair, she went to her junk drawer, searching through broken cutlery, tape, tools, and an old ball pump when her fingers slid across a battered tin box. Withdrawing it, she flipped it open with a sigh, stared at her dad's keyring to his cabin with its broken mini flashlight. Flipping it closed again, she shoved the scuffed Altoids box to the back of the drawer and found a working pen before reclaiming her seat.

Sophy.

She grabbed a bright green sticky note and wrote the name and 'mystery shifter' below it. What else did she know about her?

Sophy organized the charity event for the club.

Maybe she knew someone that could be involved? A relative or pack mate? Could she be the same woman in the club with the hyena brothers at the meeting?

She added to the note and set it aside, turning her attention back to the case files and her laptop.

There were timelines in the file for each of the robberies. Pia wanted to consolidate them all, and add to it. Where and when did it start? There was a lot of material to go through. Hare and Maliki were thorough in their work, but it would be hard to account for someone, like a shifter, that had abnormal senses and mobility, that would help them evade human investigators.

Encased in grief over her father's illness and passing since she had moved to Montreal, she hadn't done her own thorough due diligence with the job. Focus had been nearly impossible.

There were other shifters in the area—of course there were. Communities far older than the one her mother came from.

Pia sighed.

How insular had her world really become? For too long she'd been working at 20% capacity. It was time to get back in the game.

She opened a fresh table on her laptop and began the data input.

It was well past midnight when Pia straightened her spine and drew in a deep breath, rubbing her eyes. Her muscles had tightened up from the long period seated at her kitchen table, hunched over her laptop and scattered case files.

She was tired. Her mind was afire. She needed to move her body to help her brain work through the process before sleeping on it. She grabbed a pair of mostly clean shorts off the floor and slipped her feet into her running shoes. In no time she was jogging along her usual route, letting the stillness of the hour work on her. She was light on her feet so as not to wake the homeless bedded down in alleys and alcoves as she went, mindful to avoid bar districts; she needed quiet if she were to find sense in the material she was trying to chew through.

She needed to go deeper. Let her instinct work on the information for a while.

Pia found a bushy spot she used as a cache site. Glancing around her, she listened for passersby. As soon as she was satisfied that she was alone, she stepped into the shelter of the cedar bushes and stripped, setting her clothing atop her sneakers, and shifted.

Placing her paws out before her, she stretched her spine and limbs.

Ready to go, she emerged from the bushes, black fur melding into the blackest shadows of the night and set off at a trot as she let her panther take the lead. Pia retreated to the background as her panther-self stopped now and then to scent the air, tasting, processing before choosing a new direction.

Before long she found herself back in the neighborhood where the robberies had taken place. She wove her way around those same properties, avoiding the local dogs and any random skunks in the area. No time for that nonsense.

The prints she'd encountered before were all but gone as folks tended to their property, or other animals over-ran them. Any lingering scent had also disappeared in the passing days.

Nothing new to be found here. She huffed, mentally processing her route home. She'd arced around and realized the most direct route was right through Renni's neighborhood.

Was her panther instinct trying to tell her something about the case they were working, or was she trying to tell her to make a booty call? She huffed again, laughing.

How would Renni react to the sight of her, finger to the doorbell wearing nothing but the night air?

He'd probably turn tail and slam the door in her face like the stalker-panther self she was possibly becoming.

She shrugged a furry shoulder. She had to go that way, anyway, may as well do a safety run-by. Nothing to do with the fact she might spy him if there was a light on.

She was on her way home anyway.

She had to go that way.

No sense in taking the long way home, right?

She was lost in memories of Renni's hands and lips on her body as she was part way down the street from his place, and her hackles went up. She stopped and her panther growled low and deep in her throat, processing the fresh scent before Pia's distracted brain did.

Shifter.

Tangy scent.

Sophy.

Pia slowed her pace and became a moving shadow, prowling. With the stillness of the night, the scent lingered in the air. She wasn't surprised when it led right to Renni's place. However, she was surprised when it didn't lead to his front door, but around to the gate.

She didn't shift to open it. Instead, she sprang, clearing the top and landed soundlessly on the flagstones beyond it. The yard was in darkness, lit only by moonlight. She focused on the scent, following it straight to the patio door, which she realized was open.

Sophy had been here? Friendly colleague meeting? Renni had been uncomfortable when they ran into her at the shop that day. Or maybe they had a relationship he wasn't ready to give up yet, that he hadn't want her to know about?

Then realization kicked in. The door was open.

Shit.

Her head swung away from the doors toward the lounge chairs.

Shit.

Renni sat up on one, eyes wide as he stared at her. An instant later, he was on his feet.

Her gaze swept him, appreciating the lean figure in nothing but boxers. The moon accented the planes of his muscled chest, deepening the ridges.

She licked her lips, recalling the taste of his skin on her tongue and stepped forward.

He said something in Spanish and took a step back.

The scent of his fear reminded her that she was in her panther form.

Easy.

Her panther urged her forward. Pia resisted, no matter how much she wanted him.

The last thing she wanted to do was scare the shit out of him.

Panthers weren't a thing on the island of Montreal and shifting into her human self probably wouldn't be much better.

She desperately wanted to ease his fear. Her panther stubbornly put one paw in front of the other in his direction.

He stopped his backward movement, planting his bare feet on the stonework. His hands curled into fists.

He'd fight if he had to, no matter a human had little chance against the power of a panther's muscle and teeth.

She admired him for it as she noted the stance of someone who knew how to brawl.

Her panther began to purr.

Surprise flashed across his features, his posture remained the same.

The closer she moved toward him, the less she could smell Sophy. Renni filled her senses and in her panther form, it was all she could focus on. It infused her mind, imprinting. His personal musk. She touched her head to his curled fingers, arching her body against him as she swept past, dragging a deep breath of his scent across her tongue and deep into her lungs.

Renni.

His breath whooshed on a nervous laugh as his fingers loosened and flexed through the fur on her neck.

She forced herself to keep going before she did something stupid like shift and reveal herself.

With a single bound, she was over the fence and in the neighbor's yard.

Keep going, Pia.

She broke into a run, keeping to the shadows all the while, till she made it back to her cache.

Jesus fuck.

She threw her clothes and shoes back on and jogged the rest of the way home.

RENNI REPLACED THE WEIGHT bar on the brace and tilted his head so he could sit. His muscles were tight from the work out. He'd been trying to push the extra energy through his system since he'd got home after his evening out with Pia.

All he could think about was her.

When he got home, he'd wandered through his house, distracted, until he entered his office looking for something to turn his thoughts to. Flicking the light on, the file drawer, cracked open, drew his attention. He rarely opened it and kept it locked at all times. There wasn't really much of value to anyone but himself in it. He glanced around the room looking for something else out of place. Not seeing anything, he moved about the space. The safe was still locked but it was empty anyway.

He walked through the rest of the house. Nothing was missing as far as he could tell.

Maybe he'd just failed to lock the filing cabinet the last time he opened it.

He still couldn't shake the unsettled, edgy feeling colliding with the sexual energy from thinking about Pia too much. His gaze landed on the couch, where they'd had incredible sex. The memory made him harden. He grunted, removed his clothes down to his boxers and went down to the gym in the basement to work off the excess energy that was tying him in knots.

After hard rounds to push his body, he ascended to the main floor, deliberately ignored the couch and strode into the kitchen for a drink. Coconut water in hand, he approached the patio door. It was unlocked.

Was he becoming so careless, or had someone been in his house?

He remembered the news reports of robberies in his area. He had nothing of value here and nothing was missing. Maybe they'd discovered that for themselves and moved on.

For a moment, Renni's mind drifted to the past. He sighed, praying it wasn't another stalker. His thoughts instantly drifted to Sophy and quickly dismissed the notion. A fan? He hadn't received any notes or letters signaling any concerns. The stalking usually started with those before escalating.

He dismissed that too. The spotlight was finally swinging to others.

He downed the rest of the drink, set the receptacle on the counter and pushed the glass door open. He descended the terrace to the lounge chairs, settled on one parallel to the house and gazed at the stars as he relaxed.

Again, and again his thoughts returned to Pia. She was so enchanting. So unlike other women he had dated. Refreshing.

Renni had become careful. He'd learned the hard way not to give away his heart too soon. Something about Pia flew in the face of his recent years of self-isolation.

Pia was clearly a fan of the sport, but she was also a professional, a police officer. A trusted member of the community.

She seemed content to let the relationship glide, as was he. He wanted her. They were amazingly compatible in bed—such fire! And yet, where the heart was concerned, it was the slower path being tread.

Something about her drew out the desire to want more. More than just skimming along through life alone.

Still.

She could have ulterior motives he wasn't sensing.

He snorted. Sophy certainly did. She was incredibly obvious, and there was something else going on with her too, that he couldn't quite put his finger on. His instinct forced his walls up when she came around.

It was different with Pia. She seemed more the type that what you see is what you get.

Practically diamond perfect.

Of course, he could be wrong.

Subtle movement caught his eye, pulling his attention toward the house, ready to dismiss it as a tree branch shadow.

There was no wind. The night was still.

He blinked.

The black outline of a very large black cat was visible against the reflective moonlit glass of the open patio door.

A *panther*?

What the hell was a panther doing in the city?

It appeared to be looking into his house.

It moved. The large head swung toward him; luminescent eyes trained on him.

An instant later, he was on his feet, backing away several paces until his hip hit the back of the next lounge chair.

His brain struggled with coherence as it ran wild, jumping from thought to thought. Stay motionless or run like hell? Was it real or was he delusional?

It was moving toward him. He could run and jump one of the fences. So could it.

Fight then.

He clamped his lips shut. He sure as fuck wasn't going to scream. His hands curled as he braced his feet, unsure what the animal would do.

What he was not prepared for, was for the beast to start purring.

Did wildcats purr before they ate their prey?

Was this really happening?

The panther slid its head up along his knuckles, arching its back as it bumped his hand into his thigh.

He couldn't help himself as his fingers extended into its silky neck fur.

So beautiful.

Was it someone's pet?

Its throat was bare. Did people put collars on their exotic cats? If they put dresses and fancy hats on Chihuahuas, why not a panther?

Its tail curled across his abdomen like a caress.

The next he knew, the animal had bounded over the fence and was gone.

He drew in a deep breath.

Santa Madre de Dios.

He dropped onto the lounger beside him.

What a weird fucking night.

After a few moments, he rose and entered the house, ensuring the door was properly locked, and went to shower before trying to get some sleep, doubtful that he would.

TWELVE

RENNI'S EYES FOLLOWED PIA around the expanse of the ballroom at the conference center.

They'd been glued to her since he picked her up for the gala.

She'd been waiting by the steps of her apartment in the dress he'd helped her choose—the midnight blue fabric highlighted her body to perfection. With her hair in an elegant up-sweep, loose curls accentuated her delicate throat, which had a simple black ribbon tied around it. He smiled.

Perfect.

He stood between Pia and the car. "You look stunning, Pia."

She smiled, her cheeks taking on a rosy hue.

"I have something for you." He pulled a velvet box from his pocket, handing it to her.

Her brow rose as she regarded him, before popping the lid up with a gasp. Her finger trailed over the diamonds. "It's beautiful."

When her gaze turned back to his face, he could see the conflict as though she were trying to read his intentions with such a gift.

Her lips parted but Renni spoke before she could ask. "No strings. I thought it would be a lovely addition to your gown and your beauty, is all. We can discuss what to do with it later if you don't wish to keep it."

Keep it Pia, it's perfect for you.

Her eyes dropped back to the jewelry and gave a short nod. "We'll discuss it later, then."

Renni smiled *and extracted the necklace from the box. Goosebumps rose up on her skin* when *his fingers brushed her collar bones and shoulders as he put the diamonds in place. Once the clasp was locked, he caressed her nape before bending to place kisses where his fingertips had been.*

She smelled amazing. Vanilla and oranges.

His gaze landed on the top button between her shoulder blades and smiled, remembering their discussion. "I'm going to enjoy freeing your lovely body of this dress, Pia."

She turned to face him, the corner of her lips upturned, passion smoldered in her eyes.

His finger traced the necklace to the lowest point at the front. "That will remain in place, I think."

"We have to go." Her voice was a soft reminder.

Just a little taste...

He leaned down, his lips to hers. His tongue ghost-ed along her lower lip, earning an invitation. He stepped closer, she leaned into his body, her hands on his hips, his lifted to her face.

"Romantique." A voice drifted toward them.

Pia broke the kiss, turning with a smile to an older lady, frail and tiny. "Madame Cardinal."

"Une soiree?"

Pia dipped her head, then introduced Renni to the elderly woman.

Madame Cardinal's round face lit up, "Le foot-balleur. Merveilleux. Bon choix." She said to Pia and clapped her gnarled hands together in delight.

They exchanged a few more words before the elder-ly woman made her way up the steps to the building's entrance.

Renni opened the car door. Pia gracefully lowered herself onto the seat, exposing a smooth leg from within the high split in the folds of the dress.

Now, the gala was in full swing, a blur of names, faces, and jovial, strategic conversations. The auction had been a resounding success, with bidding at its highest ever for elite club access, season tickets and a specially made commemorative plaque signed by the entire team and club staff.

Pia was a welcome distraction from the chaos of the evening. Even when they weren't together, he knew where she was, his gaze always seemed to land in the right place in the room. Sensing his attention, her eyes met his.

They'd been presented as partnership between the club and the police department. Representatives of both, as they'd agreed. The media had been invited to cover the event of course, photographing and interviewing players from both local clubs, police and fire department officials, the World Association's big wigs of the sport and the flock of attending politicians.

It seemed to Renni that every time he looked up, a photographer's lens was pointed at Pia and himself at every opportunity when they were together—she was uncannily swift to turn her back on the camera. He frowned. No doubt those excess photos would be sold to the tabloids, speculating on their relationship. It had happened before. Renni had hoped a new start in a new country might be free of the tabloid world. The past always seems to find you, when you're trying to focus on the future.

Renni found his agent, Brian, who was enjoying a lively conversation.

On seeing his approach, Brian broke away from the small group.

"I'm sorry to interrupt your discussion. There is a photographer that has been too focussed on Constable Jensen when she and I are talking."

Brian frowned, turning to search the room for the photographer. "No worries, Renni, I'll go talk to them. All media were instructed to keep their photos professional and on point with the gala business."

Renni thanked him before he moved on.

Pia spoke with her precinct captain and a collection of officers and players.

As soon as she was free, he swooped in, his fingers caressing her elbow. "Breath of fresh air?"

Startled, she turned and smiled up into his face with a nod.

He glanced around to ensure they hadn't been noticed and propelled her toward a door that led through the room that stored the auction items to a small courtyard off the gallery.

Sliding his fingers along hers, they linked together, and he pulled her around along the stone path away from the doors as they enjoyed the cool night air. The courtyard was mostly in shadow, illuminated only in the central area by the moonlight.

"The media have been probing about our relationship," she said. "I need to keep as low a profile as possible. Bergeron won't like it if we end up all over the news. This is the worst place to be spotted."

Renni grunted. They had discussed the probability over their bubble tea after the dress shopping.

They were alone. Now.

Her fingers slipped to the necklace. "Renni I-"

He cut her words off with a kiss. He didn't want to talk. He wanted to taste, to rip the dress off of her and see her in nothing but that necklace and those sexy stilettos hidden under the long bell of her dress. Was she wearing panties? His mouth watered as he imagined trailing his lips along the edge of the diamonds adorning her throat to her breasts, each nipple, then down to her belly button and further still. He pulled her against him, leaving no doubt to his desire for her.

"My agent is dealing with the photographer. You're irresistible, Pia." He murmured against her ear.

She groaned, rubbing her hips against his, igniting him further so that he was ready to fuck her right there. "We should go back inside," she whispered, pulling him closer.

His lips trailed down her neck, eliciting a soft sigh from her while his hand sought the high split in the long skirt. Triumphant, his hand slid along the silky skin of her thigh, pulling her evermore closer. Fingers skipping over the lace of her thong, her heat guided him to the source of her moisture to slip inside.

"Jesus, Renni." She groaned, making his cock jerk as she began to ride his fingers. "We shouldn't be doing this here..."

He glanced up to see her eyes closed, pink tongue between parted lips.

She was so damned hot; all he could think about was sinking deep within her.

Through a haze, he realized she'd gone still, her body rigid, but not from orgasm.

She breathed into his ear. "Someone's here."

He immediately withdrew his hand to straighten her dress. He listened for a moment, not hearing anything but the steady sound of industrial air conditioners above them on the rooftops, and night traffic on the streets below. It didn't matter if it was a trick of their clandestine activities or if there had been someone, the spell was broken.

"You're sure?" he whispered back.

Her nod was sharp, her eyes trained on the shadows beyond his shoulder.

If there was someone, why hadn't they made themselves known?

The photographer.

Anger flared through him.

He spun around, keeping Pia behind him so that she would be obscured from anyone near either of the doors that opened into the small courtyard. He couldn't see anything in the darkness. After a moment she spoke again.

"They're gone."

"How do you know?"

"There was a shadow by the door that's gone now, and I heard the door click."

"Incredible hearing. Come on, we should go back inside."

THEY RETURNED TO THE main gallery. Fewer guests still lingered, networking and gossiping in clusters around the star of the evening.

The Cup.

How many business deals were born this evening?

Renni pulled Pia closer so that she could look at it, now that there was room to do so. Her smile blinded him.

"My dad would have loved to have seen this up close. Would have loved to have sat in the stands among thousands at a Global Cup game."

"I remember the sound of the crowds as we hefted it on the field after the final tournament victory. The exhilaration of knowing we were top in the world." He'd had that great privilege more than once. Every kid with aspirations to be a professional soccer player dreamed of winning that cup. It dazzled under the spotlights. The climb of his career had been to have his name associated with this prize. And he'd done it. Pride swelled his chest.

Regret threatened to twist its way through the pride, a claw to drag him down as his father flickered into his thoughts. Renni quickly boxed up the feelings and the memories and shoved them all away.

Now, he wanted to help give others the chance to touch it—to earn it, too. To give other kids a chance to train and get picked up by club scouts, as he had been. The scout that selected him for training at the club academy changed his life. This trophy was a symbol of the ultimate aspiration of a footballer—soccer player's—life. He still had to keep reminding himself that in North America it wasn't football like it was in the rest of the world. Well, excepting in those communities where the old country was still strong.

"We should organize a friendly event involving the city police, the club, and the youth—" a familiar face halted the rest of his words.

Tongue frozen, his eyes were fastened to a man that he would recognize no matter how much facial hair obscured his features. The visible skin of his face held more lines than the last time he'd seen him. The posture was unmistakable as he moved through the room, keeping his identity guarded.

Renni had seen him.

A shiver shot through his body.

"Renni?" Pia's voice drifted into his consciousness.

Renni's attention shot from the man dressed as wait staff around the room to the other figures posted in the gallery, dressed similarly.

"Renni, what's wrong?" Pia's voice was more insistent, turning to see what he was looking at.

What is he *doing here? The trophy.*

Renni moved closer to the Plexiglas case. "Where is the head of security?" He kept his voice low.

Pia scanned the room. "What do you see?" she said, her voice authoritative.

"Someone less than honest from my past. They could be armed."

"If they're armed, then someone helped them get the weapons through or around security. Are you sure?"

"Yes. These guys are dangerous."

"You have to get out of here."

He looked at her profile. She wasn't looking at him, but at the other guests.

"I'm not running away, Pia."

"Don't be macho, Renni, find a way to get the guests out without causing alarm." She said, moving toward Captain Bergeron.

Renni turned back toward the man he recognized.

Lucas Gauna.

He stood in front of Sophy with a tray of drinks for her to choose from. She said something to him that Renni couldn't hear, eliciting a quiet response and a smile. Sophy tossed her hair, as Renni had often seen her do when she was flirting with someone.

Renni moved forward when Lucas moved away. "You should think about heading home Sophy. It isn't safe here." He kept his voice low, his eyes on Lucas' back.

"What do you mean?"

"You don't want to get mixed up with that one." He nodded in Lucas' direction.

"Jealous?" She challenged him.

"Not at all. He's the kind of man you wouldn't want to be involved with."

"You know him?" She eyed him with obvious suspicion, but Renni was focused on watching the fake waiter's movements.

"Yes. You should go home; the party is wrapping up," he said with a glance round the thinning room and back to Lucas.

Lucas disappeared through a wall panel that was open for the servants to come and go. That's probably what they were waiting for—for guests to leave. Potential witnesses to leave. If they realize they've been noticed, they might get away.

He didn't bother waiting for Sophy's response. With another quick glance around the room to see if anyone was paying attention to him, he followed Lucas, who wouldn't be here alone. Maybe Renni could recognize a few more faces. He let the distance between them widen until Lucas went down a flight of stairs and around a corner.

Be careful, Renni. You told Sophy he was dangerous and while you can handle yourself in a street fight, you don't want to meet the Madre just yet, if he's armed.

He lifted his forearm to his face, exposing the crucifix hidden beneath the sleeve of his tuxedo and pressed his lips to the cross, with a few whispered words.

This couldn't be happening now, and here of all places. Lucas was supposed to be far, far away.

Renni reached the corner and eased closer to look around it. It opened into an event prep room with several more doors connected to it. There were carts loaded with empty glasses and plates pushed to the side. He glanced at the faces of the wait staff he came across, hunting for any other familiar faces. Most weren't. He recognized a few from the clubs' catering service, probably picking up extra hours.

Were any of them connected to Lucas' appearance here? He hoped not; in the months since Renni's arrival, everyone had seemed to be good folk.

He also wasn't naive. He'd grown up amid corruption. When you had a family to support, that line between corruption and survival was thin. He knew that well enough firsthand.

He moved into the room, cautious, listening.

"You should have stayed upstairs, Renni."

Renni spun at the sound of the voice he'd known most of his life. "You're a long way from home."

The other man shrugged. "You're not the only one that always wanted to see more of the world."

"What are you doing here?" Renni challenged.

"Work." He gestured to his uniform.

"Ah."

"You should go now, before you end up like your father."

Renni bristled. "I'm not going anywhere."

Lucas' eyes glittered as he stared back at Renni. "Such a poor son, you are. To abandon your father like that." He tsked.

Renni glared back at Lucas. The animosity between them had grown thick over the years.

"You're becoming more and more like Carlos."

Lucas snorted, "Of course I am, *he's* my mentor. It wasn't like *I* had a father to guide me while growing up. Someone who was willing to practically indenture himself for me." He shrugged. "Remember the streets, Renni? I'm sure you don't. A good place to learn fast."

"I remember. I remember we were friends. Family."

Lucas' lips compressed and the muscles in his jaw tightened as he swallowed. "Maybe. Maybe at one time we were. Until you left—."

Another man rushed into the room holding a cell phone, "Lucas, we have to go, they know we're here." He glanced at Renni. "*Shit*. We've got to go, man."

"Go ahead. I've been seen, so I'm going to have to take care of this."

"We were told no killing, Lucas."

"Go," he snapped at the other man, as he stepped toward Renni. "You should have stayed upstairs. Be a shame to have to do this here, but I'm not going back to prison either. And I know you won't keep your fucking mouth shut."

The other guy took one look at the handgun Lucas pulled from inside his coat and left, muttering on his way out. "I have nothing to do with this, Lucas. That's on you."

"Come on." He instructed Renni, motioning for him to move toward another door, opposite the one his accomplice fled through. Lucas pushed Renni through an outer door that opened into an alley where the convention center's trash bins were lined up.

"Why do you have to stick your nose where it doesn't belong, Renni? Last time, it got your father imprisoned. This time, well... there won't be a next time. You've been warned too many times," he said, pulling a cylinder from his pocket which he began screwing on to the barrel of the gun. A silencer.

"I can't believe you'd go after the cup. Bold even for you."

He shrugged. "Hired to do a job. Carlos pays well enough, I'll do it. Besides, like I said, I wanted to see more of the world. Nice city. Nice country. Nice women. Maybe I'll see more of it, and that pretty lady-friend of yours before I go home."

He lifted the gun, pointing it at Renni's heart.

"Leave Sophy alone."

"Sophy?" Lucas smirked. "Constable Pia Jensen, isn't that her name? Passionate, isn't she?"

Renni's eyes narrowed. "You were in the courtyard."

The gun remained steady despite Lucas' careless shrug. "Does she know?"

"Know what?"

"How crooked you are? A cop dating a crooked, selfish, *superstar*." Lucas sneered the last word. "Does she know about Carlos's grip on you? How indebted your *Papi* was to him?" his voice took on a dangerous edge.

Despite the guilt that ripped through his chest and gut, Renni said, "My father's debts were his own. They had nothing to do with me."

Lucas chuckled. "You sound so sure." He moved closer. The gun remained inches from Renni's chest.

"His debts were all about you, Renni. And you abandoned him in the end."

I know I did.

The guilt closed in on him.

Lucas wasn't wrong. He had abandoned his father.

Carlos had been very clear that Renni was to throw the game, or his father would pay the

consequences. Carlos would have made millions.

He had been prepared to do it—his father
had plead with him not to throw the game
for his sake. He would deal with the consequences of his actions. He didn't want Renni
being pulled into his dealings anymore. In the
end, his father insisted that if Renni threw the
game, his mortal soul would be tormented for
eternity. And no matter how much you distance yourself from your faith as a reasonable
adult, some things you couldn't gamble with.
And Renni wouldn't do that to his father. His
mother wouldn't have wanted it either, had she
lived.

"Did you hear me, Renni? His debts were all
about *you*." Lucas hissed; face twisted. "You owe
Carlos for this *successful* career you've had."

"What do you mean?"

Lucas' laugh was short. "It was Carlos's money
that your father used to bribe the scout for a
place in the club academy."

"You're lying." Renni spat back. He knew, deep
down, he wasn't.

Every time Renni came home for season
break, he was summoned into Carlos's presence. Carlos would inspect him, pat him on the

shoulder and tell him he was a good little foot-baller. That he made his father proud. He made Carlos proud. During those visits his father had looked anything but proud.

"That position could have belonged to any one of us playing in the street that day. Any one of us. We were all that good. It could have been mine—should have been mine. The only reason you were chosen is because your father loaded the scout's pockets with Carlos's money."

"Why didn't you ever tell me this before?" Renni snarled back.

"I didn't know until Carlos visited me in prison with the execution order. If he couldn't control you through your father, your father was no longer of use to him. Besides, he was getting old and slow—and got us caught and imprisoned." Lucas shrugged.

Liquid ice slid over Renni's scalp and down his neck and limbs.

Vaguely aware of the gun still pointed at his chest, he stared into Lucas' face and the darkness in his eyes. The darkness that had twisted since they'd last spoken to one another.

"You? My father loved you, Lucas. And you killed him?"

"It was necessary. Carlos rewarded me very well."

Renni shoved Lucas away from him. As the initial shock began to recede, he drew back his fist.

The door flew open, snapping their attention to the figure blocking the dim splash of light.

Pia.

"No!" Renni yelled as she started forward.

Lucas swung his arm in Pia's direction. Renni launched himself at him in an effort to throw his aim off. The gun fired at Pia's chest height. She wasn't there for the bullet to strike her.

Instead, a black panther launched itself in Renni and Lucas' direction.

"Shit!" Lucas yelled as jaws closed on his arm, snapping it as his finger pressed the trigger, firing off several rounds that ricocheted off the walls.

Renni, thrown to the ground by the impact, scrambled looking for Pia, who was nowhere to be seen. Her dress lay in a heap on the ground. His eyes shot back to the panther snarling in Lucas' face. A panther with Renni's diamond necklace around its neck.

"*Dios*," he breathed.

There wasn't time for more, as a growl from the other end of the alley filled the space, drawing everyone's attention. In the dull streetlight at the end of the alley, he could see the outline of what appeared to be a hyena. The second beast, teeth bared, swung its head toward Renni then jolted forward, straight for him.

Renni shot to his feet, backing away. The large cat threw itself between him and the speeding beast, sending it careening sideways with a boom as they collided with the steel trash bins lining the alley.

Lucas grabbed for his gun, which had skidded too far under the edge of one of the bins. Unable to reach it, he stumbled to his feet, clutching his injured arm, and slipped past the snarling, writhing masses of fur, muscle and teeth, running for the street.

Renni glanced back to the big black cat. The memory of his encounter with the one in his back yard flashed through his mind.

The beasts fought, powerful jaws snapping at each other, circling, blocking the exit. Renni couldn't get past them to pursue Lucas. They continued to fight between Renni and the mouth of the alley, now filled with the sounds of their snarls and snapping of teeth and rending of flesh. Sounds he'd never in his life heard before and would never forget. Primal and fierce, signaling the power of predators in full attack. The cat appeared to be wearing the powerful hyena down when two more stepped into the entrance of the alley.

"Shit." Renni breathed. He had no weapons. He dropped to his belly, reaching for Lucas' abandoned gun. It was out of his reach too. There was nothing else in the alley to defend himself with. The cat appeared to be trying to protect him. Could it hold against *three* hyenas?

The door flew open a second time to be filled with the figure of the precinct captain, gun in hand. "Christ almighty." He swore, instantly aiming at the hyenas at the far end of the alley and fired. The shots hit one in the flank and the other in the shoulder. The one engaged with the panther, wounded, backed away, then all three turned to flee.

The panther launched in pursuit.

"Constable Jensen!" the Captain's voice halted the beast.

Renni could see now how its sides heaved, glistening in the dim light. It was bleeding.

No. Not it.

The captain had named it—her.

The abandoned dress.

Her neck was bare now as he looked at her. The diamond necklace had been swiped off in the fight.

She growled low in her throat as she looked at the captain.

Frustration?

Renni eased past the panting cat toward the spot on the black asphalt that glittered and picked up the broken necklace. He noted, with some interest, how his hand shook as he held up the diamonds.

He looked up to see gold eyes trained on him. Pia's eyes trained on him.

This wasn't real.

He was going to wake up any second now.

Just a weird nightmare associated with the stress of his job and the responsibility of his role in connection to the trophy and gala.

He wasn't waking up.

Normally when a nightmare plagued him, he could break the surreal world and return to the real world.

It wasn't working now.

"Come on." The older man said, bending to retrieve the abandoned dress from the ground. He held the door open, waiting.

Renni's gaze dropped back to the large black cat, who turned her face from him and strolled inside the back door of the convention center, past the captain.

"*You*, too." The captain ordered Renni.

Numb, Renni nodded and followed the cat like it made sense to do so.

THIRTEEN

By morning, the Gala's auction success was overshadowed by the news of the bold robbery scheme, which quickly slid into speculation on Renni's involvement.

"Fading soccer star suspected of staging robbery and attack at public gala."

Pia snorted and dropped the newspaper back onto Captain Bergeron's desk. "That has got to be the most creative story headline I've ever seen come out of any newspaper claiming to not be a tabloid. At least the trophy is safe under the heavy security of the museum and league officials, as it should be."

The captain shrugged. "We still have to investigate Diaz."

She nodded.

He squinted at her. "How are you holding up? I never in my life could have dreamed I would ever see such a sight once, let alone twice. First that night down at the port, and now last night."

"Sore. The wounds are healing, I'll be fine in a couple of days." She looked at the disbelief that slid over his face when speaking of what he witnessed. "You get used to it."

"I don't know about that."

She shrugged, tugging at the collar of the spare uniform she'd kept in her locker. The restriction chaffed at her, as it never had before. Her body screamed to be out looking for the savage who'd dared point a gun at Renni, threating his life. Her panther prowled just beneath the surface of her skin.

"Any word on the other suspects?"

"The hyenas, you mean? How do my men even begin to investigate this?"

"That's what I'm here for, Captain. No, I mean the wait staff that the suspect was working with. For this kind of a job, we know he wouldn't be working alone. He isn't a shifter, he's human."

"Forensics are sweeping the alley and the club. Officers are questioning everyone that was present. Detectives are tracking everyone else's whereabouts."

Pia nodded. "Renni needs protection. The suspect was going to execute him."

The captain considered this. "He's also a suspect. We can't rule out that he isn't involved in some way."

She buried her panther's snarl.

Pia couldn't argue that, as much as she wanted to. It often happened.

"Yes, he needs to be kept under guard. Both for his protection and surveillance. I'm not going to charge him, at least not yet. I don't think he's guilty. We just have to be cautious."

"We can't keep him here. And the media are camped out at his house already," she said, gesturing at the abandoned newspaper. "Locking down a hotel floor wouldn't be much better."

"Do you really think he's still in danger?"

"Yes," she said. "The suspect was going to shoot Renni for a reason. They know each other somehow. Renni recognized him and told me to alert security."

"The suspect wouldn't want any witnesses. I'll arrange for a secured hotel room."

"I can take him somewhere they won't find him. Your men have time to investigate once Renni is finished giving his report." Pia paced the room, thinking. "Look into Sophy Khienak. After last night's encounter with a hyena shifter,

I know that's what she is now, though that doesn't automatically mean she's involved."

"The club manager's personal assistant? You mentioned before that you'd been tracking a mystery shifter involved in home robberies. Sports memorabilia." He tapped his pen on the blotter. "Makes sense to look at someone that would have access. Everyone will be questioned." He rapped the blotter again. "Do you think Diaz will go with you? The shock is probably wearing off by now."

"Renni? I guess I'll have to explain some things. He saw me. He knows it was me. I owe him something." Pia blew out a breath and crossed Bergeron's office. Exhaustion dragged at her muscles, as her brain spun with excess energy. "He may not want to see me after that."

She looked at Bergeron, who watched her with a sympathetic expression, remaining silent.

"The shifters need to be investigated. Renni also needs protection in case they go after him."

Bergeron jabbed several buttons on his phone. Dial tone buzz filled the office, punctuated by more shrill tones as he put a call in.

"Tamara Cole."

"Bergeron and Jensen here."

"What can I do for you, Captain?"

"You haven't seen the news yet?"

"I've been neck deep in work for my team."

Pia swallowed. "They're okay?"

"A lot of fires to put out, but so far, yes. Catch me up on what's going on. Last I heard everything was quiet up there in Montreal."

"It was, until a team involving hyena shifters tried to make a move on the Global Cup trophy." Bergeron said in a clipped voice.

"What is that? Is that a soccer trophy?"

"Yes, at the world level. Solid gold. Highly coveted. Worth millions."

"Perfect for black market movement."

"My gut tells me this group is connected to the robbery cases I was shadowing."

Pia repeated much of the case information for Cole as a reminder of what she'd been working on, adding the bit about a group of hyena shifters meeting and dealing locally, and they were likely the same group that came to the aid of Renni's attacker in the alley.

Sophy very well could be the woman at the hyena's meeting.

"My investigators already have boots on the ground and are working with security teams involved with the gala. Diaz has been with my men for the last couple of hours giving his statement."

Pia's gaze shot to Bergeron's face. The undertone of that meant that Renni was actually being questioned.

"So far he's been cooperative," Bergeron said, "Lucas Gauna, an Argentine national. Diaz knew him from childhood. Further investigation into Argentine media archives hints at Diaz and Gauna's connections to local crime syndicates. We're not yet clear on how they're linked."

Ice trawled through Pia's veins. Right before she'd burst into the alley, her sensitive hearing picked up raised voices through the door.

"... *It could have been mine—should have been mine. The only reason you were chosen is because your father loaded the scout's pockets with Carlos's money.*"

"I need to determine how the shifters fit into this case and how dangerous they are. This Gauna is clearly a danger to Renni." Pia said.

The captain nodded. "Jensen, keep him safe while we get this sorted out. If he's involved, and—the way things unfolded—he certainly looks suspicious, at least he'll still be in custody."

"Pia, do you have any doubts?"

"I always have doubts. My gut says Renni isn't responsible for this, but he clearly has connections to the criminal world." She drew in a breath and continued, "I'm sure it's connected to Hare and Maliki's serial robbery case. The paw prints and faint scent. Then there was Sophy Khienak's scent outside of Renni's place."

"Why haven't you mentioned *that* before now?" Cole's voice was sharp through the speaker phone.

"That could also point toward cooperation. Lovers?" Bergeron added.

Pia's stomach twisted.

"I know. Or surveillance. Could be either way. While I scented her presence, I didn't scent her *on* him." Pia said.

Bergeron nodded. "We have a forensic crew finishing up at his house. Let's see if we can lift anything of value from it. In the meantime, I want you to keep him isolated."

"I've been checking through media reports while we've been talking. Nice to see you're keeping a low profile, and not making international news, Jensen." Cole said.

She swallowed and sighed at the heavy sarcasm weighing Cole's voice.

Cole went on. "The media is insinuating you're crooked and involved in the events."

Pia glanced at Bergeron's flushed face. Apparently, he hadn't seen *those* reports.

She pinched the bridge of her nose. "I'll get it sorted out. I'm going to take Renni to a secured hotel while the local police investigate."

"You're part of that investigation now, too." Bergeron said.

Pia held Bergeron's angry gaze. She gave a sharp nod.

"We'll do what we can from here to run interference with the media if they dig too deep. Undercover is supposed to mean discrete and unseen."

Pia ground her teeth. "It was just supposed to be a community event." That she left for a few minutes, alone with him. Stupid, Pia.

"I don't know how you're going to get out of this one, Jensen. I should recall you and bury you elsewhere."

"No." She said quickly. "I'm going to figure this out. If he's involved, then he'll be exposed. If he's not, he needs exoneration. And this shifter-"

"How are you going to catch the shifter, if you're ensconced in hotel room?"

Pia bristled. Cole and Bergeron were obviously pissed. She'd promised to keep her profile low, despite their concerns of the repercussions her relationship with Renni going public would be for both organizations. "I need time to learn what I can from him. And the local PD need time to do their jobs too. Maybe they can connect Sophy to the case without exposing her true nature. Then we can take her into custody."

"We need more on her ID."

"She has no record. There hasn't been enough time to find more, but the captain has her name now, so they can dig." She glanced at Bergeron again.

He nodded.

"Captain, I'm going to have my people look into Diaz and Gauna's histories while your people work with league security on local investigations. Pia, your teammates are as deep into their cases as you are now. I'll talk to agents Maeda and Kane to see who is on standby," she said, voice tight. "Shit timing, Jensen. I'll be in touch."

The call ended.

Pia's eyes slid back to Bergeron. She straightened her shoulders.

He leaned back in his seat, folding his hands on his lap. "This isn't your fault."

Her body jerked at the unexpected acknowledgment.

"But—you said your activities wouldn't blow back on my precinct." His jaw flexed as he chewed on his thoughts before speaking. The earlier anger in his face had been replaced by weariness.

She remained silent, waiting for more.

"You'll fix this."

She nodded.

"Dismissed."

FOURTEEN

Renni rubbed his eyes as they waited for the red light to turn green.

Pia sat silent in the passenger seat of his car as they drove to his house after a long night at the police station. She was accompanying him to collect some of his things, to take while he stayed at a hotel for a few days as a precaution. After the attack in the alley, the force wanted to ensure his safety. So, this trip home was just a pit stop.

They'd already seen the news streaming across television screens, newspaper headlines and social media bursts.

Renni was on the front page.

He drew a deep breath as the light turned green, and accelerated.

Pia remained silent.

He felt her suspicion. It filled the car. Clung to him like a cloud, putting pressure on his heart.

He swallowed, sparing her a glance as he turned on to his street.

So much for trying to put his past behind him and keep it there. So much for finally taking a risk and reaching out from his place of solitude and loneliness for so long.

It had all come crashing over him like the tidal wave he'd thought had finally dissipated. It hadn't. It had only drawn back long enough to build higher and stronger.

She sat next to him in the small space, but he missed her already.

Maybe he'd imagined the part of last night where she'd turned into a cat. He'd been vague about that bit during the questioning at the precinct. What could he say? That one of their officers turned into a panther and fought a hyena in an alley in the middle of the island of Montreal? Instead, he suggested he must have hit his head during his confrontation with Lucas and that details were hazy. Which they were. His brain kept sliding away from the facts of what he'd witnessed.

Renni held on to that denial a little longer.

"Shit." Pia muttered, drawing his attention to the crowd outside his house.

He blew out a breath. As much as he had expected to see the milling crowd, he'd hoped they'd have left by now.

It was for the best that he wouldn't be staying.

His stomach dropped at the thought of them hounding the neighbors and the kids that he played soccer with in the mornings.

Dios. So much for trying to build a normal life in a new city.

There were still two cruisers parked on the street outside his house, officers monitoring events from within.

He pushed the button above his rear-view mirror. As the garage door lifted, the media spun toward his car.

Pia seemed to observe the mass with curiosity as they closed in on the car, despite its continued forward movement. Their voices infiltrated the car as they shouted over one another.

"Renni, tell us about your experiences last night."

"Renni, were you shot?"

"Who are you working with?"

"Does your girlfriend know about your past connections to the mob?"

"Did you try to steal the trophy to cover your gambling debts?"

"How long did it take you to plan the heist?"

Pia turned to him as he concentrated on easing the car through the crowd. "Are they for real?"

He nodded.

She huffed a laugh, studying him. "You're used to this."

It wasn't a question. He nodded again.

"You might be safer here than in a hotel, with all these eyes on you," she murmured as a camera was suddenly hefted in front of her face beyond the window.

She lifted her hand to shield her face from the lens, turning away from it.

Renni continued to ease the car toward the garage. The cacophony dimmed as the door closed them out.

Pia stepped between Renni and the interior door. "Wait here," she said, with one hand on the door handle, the other on her holster. "Even though officers are out front, someone could have come in the back once the forensic crew left."

Dios, she's hot. Renni couldn't stop the inappropriate thoughts from invading his brain as she eased the door open and slipped through without a sound. She returned a few moments later.

"Bergeron's crew is gone. The house is empty, but there was a shifter here recently."

"What do you mean?" Renni's veins turned to ice. "In my house?"

Pia nodded. "The scent is faint now, some-time in the last week maybe?"

"Do you know it?" he asked, tentative, curi-ous.

She gave a sharp nod followed by a shrug. "Smells like Sophy—hyena. I can't be sure it was her. There were several hyenas in that alley last night."

Renni's jaw tightened as the memory rose up in his mind.

Lucas.

And a pack of hyenas.

And Pia defending him—in a panther form.

He still wasn't sure he hadn't lost his mind. He'd been mulling over that all night, when he wasn't thinking about Lucas, and Carlos...and his father. He brushed it all away before emo-tion dragged him down. He focused on Pia.

"Well, no one is here now, so I'll just get some things. It won't take long."

Renni went up the stairs two at a time, grabbed a spare equipment bag and threw some clothes into it, followed by toiletries from the bathroom. He quickly scanned the room, trying to think of anything else he'd need as he shed the tuxedo he still wore and pulled on fresh clothes.

Packed and changed, he descended to the main floor and went to the kitchen. "Do you want a drink while we're here?" He called to Pia as he reached into the fridge to retrieve several bottles of coconut water, water and juices. He needed to flush all of last night's coffee out of his system. It was still training season after all.

Training season.

He straightened, letting the fridge door close.

How was this going to affect training and the upcoming season?

He shot a glance toward the front door, visible from where he stood in the kitchen. The media outside his house were already asking questions about his past and his participation in last night's events.

The last time he'd been dragged through a corruption investigation, it had nearly ended his career, and he'd spent the last decade clawing his way out of that black hole to the summit of his career. He doubted his career would survive another incident like that.

Fucking Carlos and his bullshit. And now Lucas too.

And this was looking bad. Very bad, if the media was already pointing fingers at him.

He'd spent most of his life trying to find distance from the criminal world. It always seemed to find him, regardless of how far he went.

Carlos ordered Lucas to kill my father.

It wasn't a prison fight.

And if Lucas was telling him the truth, then Renni's entire career had been built on his father's indentureship to Carlos. It wasn't a gambling addiction that bound his father to the crime lord. It was Renni himself.

Rage engulfed him, stealing his breath away.

Inhaling deeply, he controlled his emotions. There wasn't time for that now. Not yet.

He blew out a breath, yanked the zipper closed on his duffel bag, and strode toward the patio doors.

Pia was in the backyard, facing the hedges between the properties.

He slid the door open and stepped out. "Everything all right?"

She turned toward him, lips quirked, and nodded.

Ella squeezed between the cedar branches, popping out the last few inches. "Renni!" she cheered, stumbled to catch her balance, then launched herself at him.

He hauled her up into his arms as her little ones wrapped around his neck with an unexpectedly vise like grip.

"I thought you were hurt," she said in her usual rushed way. "Those news people have been saying all kinds of things about you. They think you did something bad. But I know you don't do bad things, right Renni?"

His heart dropped. "Right, little one."

"Why would they say you did?"

"They're looking for stories to tell." Pia said.

"I don't like their stories." Ella frowned.

"Have they been bothering your family?" Renni asked her.

She nodded.

Anger flared through Renni's chest a second time. He tightened his arms around her.

Before he could ask her anything else, she turned her gaze to Pia. Speaking to Renni, she said, "I like her more than the other lady that was here. I like her uniform. Is your gun heavy?" She asked, switching her focus.

Pia smiled. "Yes, but not too much so that I can't handle it."

"Can I-"

"Nope. No one touches a police officer's weapon, except the officer that is responsible for it."

Ella sighed, letting her interrupted question go.

"What other lady?" Renni asked Ella.

"The lady that came to visit you at night. I couldn't sleep, so I was on my balcony with my doll and your lady friend came in through the gate and went in through the patio doors. Don't you remember?"

Renni shook his head. "I don't think I was home, *Cara*, the only lady that's visited me here is Pia."

Pia pulled her phone from her pocket.

"You were home, I saw you in the backyard afterward. The same night the big kitty visited you."

His attention shot to Pia, whose cheeks pinked, despite her schooled expression.

Renni was taken aback by just how much his little neighbor knew about what was happening in his backyard. He was suddenly very thankful he'd never gone skinny dipping or nude sun-bathing.

"Ella, do you remember what the lady looked like?"

The little girl nodded.

Pia held up her phone so that Ella and Renni could see the screen. A group photo from the previous night's gala included Renni and Pia along with a couple dozen other people from the club, the organization and the department. "Is she in this photo?"

Ella's little fingers poked the screen, double tapping to make the faces bigger, then moved it around as she looked at the faces. "*This* one looks like her."

Renni peered at Sophy's smiling face, half obscured by Ella's finger.

Damnit.

"And this man. I saw him another time." She pointed at a man dressed in wait staff attire standing off to the side, separate from the group.

Renni sucked in a breath. "Lucas." His gaze shot to Pia's face.

"Listen," he said to Ella. "You shouldn't be out on your balcony when your Momma or Pappa isn't with you, *Cara*. Some people aren't nice, and if they know you see them, and they're doing something they aren't supposed to, they might do something mean."

Ella's eyes widened.

Pia held out her hand for the phone, which Ella gave back to her.

"Ella? Ella, where are you?" Ella's head turned toward the sound of her mother's worried voice.

"I'm here, mommy."

Renni let her down when she squirmed to free herself and she ran back toward the hedge.

"Ella, I told you not to go over there anymore."

"But Mommy, I-"

"No, Ella." Her voice was hard, allowing no room for argument.

Ella turned sad eyes on Renni and Pia, then waved before squeezing back through the shrubs to her own property.

"We should go." Pia said.

Renni finally pulled his gaze from the bushes, heart heavy, nodded, and turned to go back into the house.

FIFTEEN

BACK AT THE STATION, Pia had relayed the information that Ella had witnessed Sophy and Lucas at Renni's place to Captain Bergeron, corroborating the extra information to focus the investigation on these individuals for suspicious behavior around a private residence.

Then, they had driven Pia's car to the hotel where he was to stay for a couple of days, until the media found someone else to focus on and the police were able to locate Lucas and his accomplices.

They'd been in the hotel room for a few hours already, with two officers posted in the hall to deter any unwanted visitors.

Renni had been pacing the suite for the last twenty minutes. The steady tread of his feet lulled Pia's attention away from listening to the sounds beyond their room. There was little movement in the hall, mostly the shuffle and low talking of the police guards posted outside the door.

One ribbed the other over his choice of baseball cap.

"It's good luck, there's a game tonight."

Every now and then the elevator doors would open, with quiet footsteps trailing down the hall opposite their position.

Pia looked up from the report she'd been typing up on her laptop, eyes following Renni.

She understood the feeling of being caged. She could feel it prickle beneath her skin, too. She was also used to confinement for long periods of time while working on a case.

Renni glanced in her direction and offered a wan smile when he noticed her attention on him. "I'm usually in training with the team right now."

It had been taking everything she had to keep her focus on the reports, and not let her thoughts drift to the bed, visible through the door dividing the bedroom from the sitting area of the suite.

Even the couch was bringing back memories of Renni's sculpted body under hers as she rode him.

He resumed pacing, his muscles taut under the fabric of his shirt and pants. She licked her lips, thinking of peeling them from his body.

Now isn't the time for distractions.

Her body didn't care that he could possibly be involved in the robbery. She still wanted him. Her cop/GPSA brain told her to maintain her suspicions, while her gut told her he was innocent—despite the fact that it also told her he was hiding something.

Maybe just a few minutes of distractions...

All three were at war with one another, and in the meantime, she decided that letting her eyes have free reign while her brain, gut and body duked it out was totally okay.

Plus, she was stalling. Putting plenty of space between herself and the conversation that was bound to happen.

Besides, she doubted he'd want her now that he knew she was a shifter. One of the reasons she stayed the hell out of long-term relationships with humans was that once the human found out she wasn't as human as they were, they back-pedaled on their protestations of undying love pretty damned fast.

Her body said she didn't need professions of love.

Her brain told her to keep her distance.

Her gut and heart and kitty said he was the one.

Holy hell, what?

No.

Pia refused to believe in that shit, so where the hell had that come from?

Maybe some couples were mated for life. As far as Pia was concerned, if her parents couldn't make it work, regardless of how much they loved each other, then it was just total luck for some.

She died, Pia. It wasn't like she left him.

Whatever.

Her parents didn't live happily ever after.

It wasn't going to happen for her either.

She never believed it would, so, she always shunted it from her mind... and her plans.

A barrage of images of Renni slugged her hard.

Naked. Laughing. Concentrating. Cooking. Loving her. Holding Ella in his arms...

She barely knew him.

The direction these thoughts were going was dangerous. Too dangerous.

No, Kitty.

"Pia?"

She blinked.

Renni was staring at her. "You okay?"

"Uhm, yeah, just thinking."

Her stomach made a loud growling noise at that moment, filling the space.

Renni smiled. "I'm hungry, too."

"I'll order room service," Pia said, and got up to grab the hotel restaurant menu.

She called in the order, closed her laptop, and slid it back into her bag to make room for the food on the table once it arrived.

She glanced up and found him staring at her again.

"What is it?"

He shrugged and turned back to the windows overlooking the downtown core.

She moved to stand next to him, taking in the view of the city below. The summer sun glinted off skyscrapers and the river in the distance and gave the old stone buildings a warm tint. She looked down on the streets she'd become so familiar with in the last year. If she hadn't transferred here to spend the last months of her father's life with him, where would she be now?

A knock sounded on the door, drawing her attention.

She hesitated, glancing at the clock on the desk. And listened a moment.

Had it been long enough for the food to be prepared? They hadn't ordered much.

She couldn't hear anything coming from the hall outside the door.

She'd been distracted and couldn't recall if she'd heard the elevator doors.

Pia waved Renni to move into the suite's bedroom, pulling the door closed behind him, before approaching the main door. If the media had somehow got past the guards, she wasn't going to have them snap shots of him. Or worse, one of Gauna's men snapping shots, either.

The knock sounded again.

An officer should have alerted her to who was at the door.

She unclasped her gun, easing her fingers around the handle.

A third knock came.

"Who's there?" she called, moving soundlessly behind the door, easing up onto tip toe to see out of the peephole. Whoever was there was just out of its line of sight.

"Room service."

"I'm not dressed, just leave it by the door."

There was a pause. "I need you to sign for it."

"Have the officer on duty sign for it and leave it by the door."

"There's no one else here."

She froze.

There should be two officers monitoring the door.

Had they been drawn away?

Were they injured?

Why hadn't she heard anything?

Goddessdamnit, she'd been distracted by Renni's lovely posterior. Having her eyes full didn't make her fucking deaf.

Scenarios rolled through her mind as to what could have happened.

She wasn't fully suited. Just the basics and her weapon. She should have grabbed a vest from her car.

Pia considered her options. Shift and potentially tangle in her clothes before she could attack, or fight in human form with her gun, fists and feet.

Her eyes trained on the floor, watching the slide of light and shadow under the crack of the door.

Pressing her ear to the door, breath held, she heard the distinct sound of a mechanism clicking into place before the first distinct sound of silenced gunfire cracked into the door next to her.

Instinct triggered her reflexes, bouncing her back out of the way before the next shots could make it through the door itself.

She backed to the suite's bedroom door and shouted at Renni. "Call the police," she said, holding up her gun, aimed at the main entry point, ready for it to be breached.

The door handle turned and eased open with two men wearing latex gloves lurking in the doorway, guns aimed at Pia.

Her eyes dropped to the figure lying on the floor just beyond the door.

"He's unconscious. We're not cop killers unless we have to be. Put your gun down."

Pia sniffed.

Humans.

How the hell had they incapacitated both police officers without her hearing anything?

Organized.

"We're just here for Diaz, sweetheart. Hand him over and you'll gain nothing more than a little bump on the head."

The scent of chloroform drifted toward her nose through the open door.

Through the bedroom door, she heard Renni speaking to the 911 dispatch.

"What makes you think I'll hand him over?"

The taller of the two laughed, looking her up and down.

She grinned back at his arrogant stance.

"Be careful Rod, she looks like one of those crazy bitches."

She tilted her gun so that it was aimed at the taller one's head. He took a step back.

Rod continued to move forward, widening his approach. "You can only shoot one of us, sweetheart."

"You sure about that?"

Rod blinked, uncertainty crossed his features. He continued to move further to her right. The scent of chloroform intensified as he approached. He'd exchanged his gun for a wad of some kind of fabric that seemed to be the source of the chemical.

She let him move in closer.

The taller guy still had his gun trained on her as he waited for his partner to drug her.

In the bedroom, Renni was silent.

Stay where you are.

If anytime was a good time to suddenly develop telepathy, now would be great.

She eased her weight a fraction, turning more toward Rod. Her gun remained pointed at the taller guy.

"Careful Rod, she's going to shoot both of us."

"I didn't say that." Her eyes flicked between the too. "I just asked if you were sure I couldn't."

As soon as Rod was in position and close enough to reach for her, she let him.

Her body tightened, ready to spring.

Rod darted toward her shoulder, arms spread to encircle her and get the doused fabric toward her face.

A second later, she jabbed her elbow back into his solar plexus, taking the wind out of his gut and setting him off balance. Another second and she was the one with her arms around him, her free hand pressing his gloved hand to his own face. Her gun remained pointed at the taller guy who gaped, but maintained his stance. Rod struggled, unable to break her hold on him.

"You really are a crazy bitch." The taller guy said.

"You know, most ladies really, really, hate that term."

Rod's body went slack, and she dropped him in front of the threshold of the bedroom door, where she'd been standing. She eased back and away, holding the taller goon's attention. Their guns remained pointed at each other.

She could take a bullet if she had to. It would hurt like fuck and slow her down a little. It wouldn't kill her—unless he shot her in the head or heart.

Sirens echoed off the concrete and glass. The criminal's eyes flicked toward the window.

"They'll be here soon. Then you'll be surrounded."

"And I won't be here."

"You sure about that?" she said again.

His eyes swiveled to his downed partner. He shrugged his large shoulders, the tension in his body clear. "Yeah." He lied. She smelled his rising fear.

She took another step. They were now positioned so that he was between the bedroom door and herself, now closer to the exit.

He stepped toward her.

Renni opened the bedroom door.

The man swung his gun toward Renni who stepped back and raised his hands.

Pia darted forward several steps.

The man's gun returned its aim at to her. "Mr. Diaz, I'm here to take you to talk to Mr. Gauna. If you come with me, no one will get hurt."

"Alright, just let me get my bag. Just don't shoot."

"Leave it." The man said, but Renni had already stepped back into the room.

"You'll carry it for me, right?" Renni said, appearing in the doorway again. As soon as the man's attention turned back toward Renni, Renni threw the duffle bag at his face.

The man reflexively brought his hands in to stop the bag from hitting him and Renni launched himself forward, throwing his entire body against his to bring him to the floor. The gun fell away as they struggled.

Pia darted forward to retrieved it. "That's enough."

The men struggled to overpower each other a few heartbeats longer—until Pia cocked the attacker's gun, pointing it down into his face.

Frozen, he looked up at her, daring her to shoot him.

The blare of sirens in the street below, cut out. The cavalry had arrived.

"Renni, grab the cuffs from the officers in the hall."

Back on his feet, he did as she asked. Pia handed Renni the second gun while she pushed the conscious attacker over with her foot and secured his hands behind his back with her cuffs, then did the same with his partner using the cuffs Renni handed to her. She then patted them both down, checking pockets and boots for hidden weapons, confiscating anything she found. Rod had some zip-ties tucked away that Pia used to tie the men's cuffs to each other, making it harder to move. Then used the zip-ties to do some fancy loop and tie knots to secure their ankles to each other.

"Let's go," she said, scooping up Renni's bag from the floor and tossing it to him before grabbing her own.

On their way out of the room, she crouched beside one of the officers that had been wearing a baseball cap. "Here," she tossed it to Renni. "You're too recognizable with all that hair.

"I hate hats, they look terrible on me." He said as they by-passed the elevator toward the stairwell.

Pia paused at the fire door to look at him, rolling her eyes, "Honey, you look hot no matter what you're wearing. Just put it on."

"You think so?" he grinned at her.

Shoving the door open. "Seriously? You've just had two goons try to kidnap you and you're worried what people will think of how you look?"

"Just you."

She paused before descending the next flight of stairs. He grinned at her.

Pia couldn't help herself and grinned back. "Like I said. You could wear anything... or nothing. We have more pressing things to worry about." She continued down the stairs.

"I was thinking about cutting my hair anyway, time for a change."

"Really? Isn't your hair part of your signature look?"

"Like I said, time for a change. Maybe time to grow up a little."

Pia reached the basement door. Glancing over her shoulder at Renni, she considered. "I'm sure a haircut would be just fine." She held a finger to her lips as she eased the door open, listening.

Poking her head through the open door, the parking garage appeared to be empty. They ran to her car, throwing the bags in the backseat.

As soon as the doors were closed, Renni asked her, "why aren't we meeting with the incoming police?"

"Those two might not have come alone. Best to get out of here unseen, if we can. I'll contact the captain later." She started the car, threw it into gear and eased toward the garage exit.

SIXTEEN

Pia and Renni drove straight for her apartment.

"Wait here," she said, parking part way down the block. "I'm going to grab a few things from my place."

By the time she reached the front steps, Madame Cardinal was struggling with her grocery cart. Pia lifted the cart one handed while slipping the other under the older lady's arm to help her up the steps.

"Oh, hello my dear!" she said in French. "I'm so happy to see you've finally decided to have some friends over to your home. It's good for you to socialize." She scrunched up her face in a smile.

"There are some friends waiting for me?"

"Oh, I don't know. Some men came by looking for you earlier as I was leaving to do my shopping. They said they were here to take you and your friend Renni Diaz out. He is very handsome. You will have to tell me how you met."

Pia's heart was pounding in her ears, mind racing as she carefully eased the frail old woman toward the elevator, deciding to escort her safely to her apartment, in case the men were still there. No shifter scents lingered in the narrow space.

The doors slid open, and they stepped out. Pia moved to match Madame Cardinal's slow pace along the short alcove where the elevator bank was connected to the main hall. At the corner, she eased forward, glancing in both directions. She drew a breath, letting it out through her lips.

Madame Cardinal looked up at her as she unlocked her apartment door. "You're very tense. You deserve a fun night out with your friends."

"I sure do." She smiled as they went inside. Pia pulled the grocery cart toward the kitchen and unloaded the groceries as quickly as she could, as she'd often done in the past. By the time she finished, the older woman had her coat hung up and the kettle boiling. "Listen, my friends can be a little rowdy sometimes. Best you stay in here if you hear any noise coming from my end of the hall."

Madame Cardinal chuckled. "Should I call the police if there is too much after hours noise?" her eyes twinkled as she looked point-edly at Pia's uniform.

"Absolutely." She smiled back. "And especially don't let my friends in if they come knocking on your door. They'd probably have had too much too drink, and just be up to mischief."

As soon as the elderly neighbor was settled into her home, Pia left for her own apartment on silent feet. The scents lingering around her door were human. Different from the two at the hotel. A big operation?

Pressing her ear to the door, she listened.

No sounds were audible beyond the wood. The door appeared to be undamaged. She slid the key into the lock and eased the door open, ever cautious.

Hand on her weapon, she stepped into her home and sucked in a breath.

The heavy scents of exertion and frustration coated her tongue as she glared at the mess of her personal space.

She'd been called to many break-ins during her career. She'd been covering the robberies and been witness to the roll of emotions the victims went through. As sympathetic as she could be, this was the first time she'd experienced that kind of violation of space firsthand.

Her kitty snarled at the invasion of her territory.

She couldn't imagine what they were looking for in her apartment. She had nothing of value. Regardless, they must have guessed she'd be the one working Renni's case. She strode past the discarded and overturned drawers, resisting the instinct to fix them—to put her things back in their place, continuing to her bedroom. It hadn't been spared either. She swallowed the revulsion as she surveyed the clothing dumped on the bed and the knowledge someone had had their hands on her personal belongings. Stepping around the bed, she moved toward the window, glancing out to see if she could spot anyone watching the building, then up the street toward her car. Her enhanced sight allowed her to see that Renni was still there.

Ignoring the chaos of her space, she grabbed a spare bag from where it had been tossed, inside out in the corner, and grabbed handfuls of clothes, stuffing them in. She'd call the Captain from her car.

The kitchen was just as wrecked at the rest of the place. Her usual workspace at the table lay in turmoil. Even her father's estate papers littered the space.

Rage, sudden and violent, ripped through her chest, stealing her breath.

The bag dropped from her hands; all thoughts muffled as the urge to right the little stack of paper took over as grief muted logic. Her hands shook, papers clutched between them, chest heaving as though she'd been sprinting rather than just collecting feather light sheets of paper.

She reached for a file folder to slide them into, when realization struggled through the brain fog.

The robbery case files she'd been keeping were gone. The empty folder in her hand was from one of them.

Pia closed her eyes, drawing a shaking breath to try to dispel the unexpected onslaught of grief that overwhelmed her.

Between the media surrounding Renni's place, the attack at the hotel and the invasion of her apartment, it seemed both of their lives were about to be a whole lot more exposed to the world.

Pia turned back to the emptied kitchen drawers for the contents of the 'junk drawer'. Spotting the battered tin Altoids box, she snatched it up, checking that it still held the keys she'd hidden in it, stuffed it in her pocket, then left her apartment.

"Well, we're definitely not staying at my place," she said as she got back into the car, tossing her bag onto the backseat next to her laptop bag and Renni's duffel bag. She placed the folder with her father's estate papers on the floor behind her.

She slipped her earpiece in place, dialed the captain's number on her cell, turned on the car, and sped toward the highway entrance, filling him in on everything that had happened in the last thirty minutes, including the fact they'd taken her work on the robberies. She knew by now there'd be a police crew investigating the hotel scene. Now they just needed to send someone to her apartment.

Maybe they could lift some prints.

She doubted it. These guys were experienced enough not to leave any behind.

PIA GLANCED AT RENNI, who had remained silent for the duration of the drive north on Highway 15. Once she was sure no one had followed them out of the city, she eased her shoulders a fraction as they made the turn onto the 333 and pulled up to a grocery store.

"Stay here, in case anyone recognizes you." She unclipped her seatbelt, finally turning her attention full on him. He didn't look at her. "Do you want anything from inside?"

He shook his head, watching a family exit the store, cart loaded with groceries and kids. "They might recognize you, too," he said.

"Less likely. Keep the doors locked, I won't be long." She stood outside the car, pretending to check her hair and makeup while scanning the lot, noting the dozen or so cars and trucks, spared a quick glance at the small gas station across the road, then went inside. She grabbed the most basic fare. Pia didn't care if she had to eat peanut butter sandwiches for a few days. Renni hadn't requested anything, and she didn't know what to buy for him. They just didn't know each other well enough. That wasn't totally true. She suspected he might not be so partial to days and days of peanut butter. She shrugged. No time to worry about that. At least there would be coffee. She sighed, sped up and down the aisles and around the cold foods perimeter, tossing things almost at random into her cart.

She didn't even know how long they'd be there. Hopefully not long. Renni's silence was already getting under her skin. Was he worried about spending a few days alone in the mountains now that he knew her alter ego was a wild animal? She quickly threw that thought out of her mind. She needed to focus on her job. He was a person that needed protecting and she needed to be professional about the situation.

She paid for the groceries and loaded them into the trunk, doing another scan of the parking lot as she did so, noting two potential tails. One parked by the gas station ice fridge, the other at an angle toward the rear of the grocery lot with the driver speaking on a cell phone. Tinted windows and sun glare made it difficult to glean any details.

Renni still didn't say anything to her when she got back into the car, with a glance to ensure he was still alone.

"We're going to take the long way around the lake." She started the car and eased back onto the northbound lane. She pulled a packet of gum from her pocket, popped two out of the plastic and foil, then dropped it into the empty cup holder. "For the elevation."

He glanced at the rising landscape and picked it up.

Pia accelerated, her attention as much on her rear-view mirror as on the road ahead. Both cars she'd noticed pulled onto the road several car lengths behind them. By passing the turn to the cottage, she kept going until they made it to the tiny village of St. Hippolyte. As soon as they went through the stop sign and down the hill, which was sharp enough to obscure them from followers for a few seconds, she made the abrupt turn into the busy church parking lot. She swung the car into one of the few empty spaces with the nose of the car pointing back toward the road. It seemed an eternity before one of the trailing cars rolled by the church property. The second car didn't pass by.

They waited for another quarter hour, until the service finished and the parishioners emerged from the building, and filed out of the parking lot along with them before continuing the drive to the cottage. The narrow road wove and undulated along the mountain face, oncoming traffic whizzing past like roller-coaster cars. All the while, Renni remained silent, eyes trained on the windshield, hands resting on his thighs.

She made the quick turn onto the ever-narrowing dirt road, then crossed a picturesque, rushing mountain creek on a wood and steel beam bridge. After several kilometers of continuous climbing, she stopped at the head of the driveway, which seemed to drop 10 feet, over-looking nothing but treetops. Leaving the car running, she and Renni got out and they unloaded the trunk's contents at the top of a series of wooden staircases that descended to a platform below. Dropping the trunk lid, she proceeded to back the car into the corner of the lot, where it would be sheltered from view of the road by exposed rock and overhanging trees. Renni had all of the heavier bags in hand, leaving Pia only her small pack and some of the smaller bags.

She led the way down the winding steps toward a cabin nestled three-quarters of the way down from the clifftop parking lot. Descending the final few steps toward the patio doors, she set her bags down, extracted a key from her pocket and made her way around to the front of the small house. Once inside, she let Renni in through the sliding doors where she'd left the bags, then went to check on the power and septic systems. By the time she returned, Renni had almost finished putting the groceries away.

"Lucas won't let this go."

After the maintained silence of the drive, the sudden sound of his voice in the small space startled her.

She shrugged. "I doubt he'll find us out here. I plan to patrol every night anyway. Coffee?" She pulled the coffee grinder from the cupboard and plugged it in. "We need to talk." She said, punctuating her frustration by mashing the button with her finger, setting the grinder to work while she filled the coffee machine's water reservoir.

She glanced over her shoulder to see Renni standing in front of the window that ran the width of the tiny kitchen, overlooking the lake.

The grinder whined to a stop, pulling her attention back to the task. While the coffee brewed, she considered how to broach the subjects they needed to discuss. Shifters and his connection to Lucas and the crime world.

She had no doubt that had been his first encounter with a shifter, and the likely reason for his silence. Pia was used to that. It didn't negate the sting of rejection. It was familiar ground. She could use it to maintain the distance that had cracked its gaping maw between them, and distract her from the feelings that had been building for him. She'd been falling for him, but hadn't allowed herself that last tip over the edge. Thank Goddess for that.

At the hotel, she'd slipped.

Now she needed to consider him as just a charge. Another protection detail. Simple. Easy.

That's the mantra she would use to convince herself.

Her eyes swept the back of him. Her throat tightened on a lump. Probably a little piece of her heart trying to jump ship.

SEVENTEEN

"WE NEED TO TALK," Pia said, before starting the grinder.

Renni waited, staring out of the window overlooking a perfect scene of the lake. He lost himself in the view for a few minutes, still trying to find his equilibrium and rational brain after the events of the last 24 hours.

Talk?

They'd gone from enjoying each other's company at a public charity event to Renni suddenly seeing wild animals fighting in a back alley.

The woman he'd been falling for *was* one of those wild animals.

And he *was* falling—no, *did* fall—for her, despite repeatedly telling her there were no strings attached.

I've made a liar out of myself.

Just because he felt that way about her, didn't mean she reciprocated—or needed to.

His mind kept returning to the night he'd seen the panther in his backyard, trying to match the two together and understand it all. What did it mean? Anything?

And Lucas' sudden appearance here in Montreal? The last thing in the world he'd expected—aside from human-animal-hybrids—was the appearance of his old friend at that gala.

The animal-thing he could try to chalk up to a delusion of some kind. Maybe there'd been a gas leak in the building, or someone spiked the drinks. Anything.

He glanced at Pia. No. It was real.

He couldn't dismiss this.

What had it cost her? To reveal her secret in order to protect him from a loaded weapon?

Seeing Lucas there, in that building, and then actually pointing a gun in his face? Things had become strained over the years, but to the extreme that Lucas wanted to *kill* him?

All because Renni's father had bribed a scout, what? Twenty years in the past?

Pain stabbed at Renni's chest. He drew a deep breath and rubbed his hands over his face as his gut twisted.

While he faced the serene lake before him, his mind was in turmoil.

Jealousy between brothers.

No. Not brothers anymore. Not for a long time, if Renni was finally honest with himself. That time, on the streets—those memories were nothing but nostalgia. A memory to hold on to during the upheaval of life in those early days when he'd left home to join the academy and his whole world had veered sharply and permanently toward a life of his dreams.

Time to let the past go.

Lucas was no longer his street-brother. He was his enemy. An enemy that hated him so much he was prepared to kill him. An enemy that had killed Renni's father, a man that had loved Lucas as one of his own.

He let the last vestiges of the past fall away. Lucas was dangerous. Was the hit on Renni also one of Carlos's orders? No. The look in Lucas' eyes told him this wasn't business. It was personal.

Renni had pursued Lucas out of that ballroom. Opportunity. Perhaps. Given the exchange in that alley, he had no doubt Lucas would have come after him at some point after the job of stealing the trophy was done.

He drew in another deep breath. It didn't matter if Carlos called it or Lucas. If Renni was in their crosshairs, then anyone around him was also in danger. They would do anything they could to drag him down and isolate him. It wouldn't be the first time.

The media was going to be bloated with the fodder of Renni's personal life for months. His contract with the club would end since he'd instantly become an extreme liability rather than an asset.

And the attack at the hotel. They'd gone there to avoid the media and been met with Carlos's men going after them. Even Pia's apartment wasn't safe. They'd been followed out of the city, could whoever that was track them here?

Pia wasn't safe.

He'd spent his entire life trying to keep a distinct separation between his childhood and his career. He'd been kidding himself. Carlos had always had his hand in things.

Looked like Renni couldn't deny his ties to the past any longer.

"Where do you want to start?" He finally said, turning to look at Pia as she placed a mug of coffee on the wooden table between them.

She straightened with a shrug.

He decided to go for the easier, more ridiculous topic. "That wasn't real, was it? The animals?"

He was grasping. The more he thought about what happened, it was harder to deny.

Pia stiffened, sipped her coffee, her eyes steady on him over the rim.

Finally, she said, "it was real."

"You... you're a panther."

She nodded. He noted the rise in color of her normally creamy skin, her expression remained mask-like.

Renni couldn't think straight. Lack of sleep, and shock, tended to do that. He picked up the mug and drank half the coffee despite the scalding heat. "That was you—at my house."

She nodded again.

"Why?"

"I'm an agent for the Global Paranormal Security Agency embedded in the Montreal precinct to help the regional authority with paranormal criminals crossing borders." She straightened her shoulders as she leaned back against the kitchen counter. "I was in the area, scouting a case close to your place, and... had to bypass your neighborhood on my way home when I caught a scent down the street from your house that led right to your back door."

He froze as ice rippled its way down his spine and along his arms. "Scent?"

She seemed to consider what she was about to say next. "The same scent I picked up from your colleague in the dress shop."

He thought back. "Sophy." He blew out another breath. "I'd forgotten that Ella said that she'd seen her on my property—and that you said you smelled her in my house."

Pia nodded.

He suppressed a shudder.

"Are you sleeping with her too?"

Dios, what? Her words snapped him upright. "No."

"She is beautiful. Would make sense for her scent to be at your house."

"No. I've never invited her to my home." A pit was forming in his gut.

His instinct and glimpses into her personality had forced him to keep his distance from her. He'd brushed away thoughts of the idea that she was stalking him. His filing cabinet had been open, and the patio door had been unlocked the night the panther came through his backyard. "So, she is one of them? One of the hyenas that protected Lucas. Is she the one you fought?"

Pia shook her head. "Those were all male hyenas in that alley. I'm sure she's connected to them in some way. Exactly *how*, I don't know yet. Maybe a pack mate." She shrugged. "I was hoping you might be able to offer something."

"I don't know her, not really. She arrived at the club shortly after I did. Tried to gain my attention, but I wasn't interested. She's been persistent in trying to spotlight me in the club events. Single me out."

"Why not?"

"Ask her out? Instinct. My gut told me that route was trouble. Besides, I didn't like how she treated the club staff."

Pia raised a brow.

Renni finished the coffee in his mug. "I don't like people that act sweet to those in positions of authority, then mistreat those they think are below them. I've seen it too many times in this industry. As soon as they get another step up, they have another layer below them to treat with disdain."

"Opportunists."

"More than that." He put the mug down. "That kind of narcissistic manipulation disgusts me.

Every single one of the folks that work for that club works hard and no one deserves to be treated like 'less than'. The team is so much bigger than just the players."

The tightness in his chest eased as he said the words. Rosa's smiling face drifted into his thoughts. Maintaining political balance in the workplace was precarious with so many egos running the place.

"Tell me about Lucas."

"We grew up together. Spent our days with the other neighborhood kids playing in the streets."

"Where you learned to play soccer."

He nodded.

"And also learned how to fight?"

"As we got older, our friendly games often turned into brawls—serious brawls." He shrugged. "Passion for the sport."

Pia's head tilted as she regarded him.

"And how often were you on the wrong side of the law?"

He flinched.

There it was.

"It's a thin line, depending on what neighborhood you're in."

"Lucas Gauna and Carlos Moreno."

"Long story."

"We have a little time." She pushed herself up onto the countertop, letting her feet dangle. Her eyes remained pinned to his face.

Renni leaned against the wall next to the picture window, turning his back on the lovely view of the lake, crossing his ankles and arms, returning Pia's direct stare. "Carlos Moreno has his thumb on everyone in that neighborhood. He rules it."

"The police don't get involved," she said.

Renni nodded. "They have their understandings."

"I'd read that your father had some shady connections that caused some trouble for you early on in your career."

"Yes."

"Like bribery."

"Apparently."

She raised a brow, waiting.

He uncrossed his arms, scrubbed his face again and recrossed them. He stared at his shoes for a long moment before returning to Pia's impassive face.

He'd grown used to being able to read her. Now, he couldn't.

Nor could he summon the words to speak aloud what he never had before. His gut churned. Heat rose up his neck as he found a place to start. His gaze dropped to the scarred pine floor. "I always thought my father had a severe gambling addiction. He never seemed able to settle his debt with Carlos. My whole life..." He drew another breath, the tension easing in increments as the words fell out. "My whole life, we were tied to Carlos. And my father always let me believe it was his fault... but it wasn't. It was mine."

"How so?" Pia's voice was curious, tight.

He looked at her again. "Lucas told me... last night, that my father bribed the scout to get me into that training academy. With money he borrowed from Carlos to do it."

"You believe him?"

Renni nodded.

"And Carlos never seemed to let him pay it off?"

Renni nodded. "That never ending debt caused a lot of tension between us. As much as I loved my father, I also hated him for that constant point of pressure from Carlos. No matter how much money I gave my father to pay his debts, the debts just seemed to grow. And

I could never understand why. Even when I forced him into rehabilitation for gambling."

Renni slid down the wall to sit on the floor. "Now I also understand why he was so adamant that I did not throw that game." He dropped his head toward his knees, lacing his fingers across the back of his neck.

"You threw a game?" Pia sounded incredulous.

"No. Almost. But no."

"What happened?" her voice softened, encouraging him to confess.

He returned his attention to her face. Her expression wasn't hard and judgmental, as he had expected. It was full of compassion.

"Carlos was hinting *real* hard—in his Carlos Moreno way—that he would greatly benefit from a particularly high stakes game if the match was won by the other team. Not just how he would benefit. How my father wouldn't suffer the consequences if I allowed the game to go any other way than what Carlos predicted it would."

"That's awful." She whispered.

"I'd never, ever seen my father beg until that day. He came to see me before the game and begged me not to do it. Not to jeopardize my career. That no matter how tied to Carlos he was, that I should not be. He made me promise to keep the game honest and to request a transfer to Europe."

"And Carlos lost money."

"A lot of it."

"According to the articles I read, your father went to jail shortly after you went to Europe."

"Yes. He was forced to work off the money Carlos lost, doing shit jobs—robberies, shake ups, whatever Carlos told him to do. Then one time, I guess the job went wrong and my father and Lucas were arrested. Carlos had them working together. It was obvious Lucas was being groomed and already in deep by then. I don't know all the details. Just what my dad told me in his letters, which wasn't much. You learn to read between the lines."

"You never went back?"

"My father was adamant I stay away."

"That must have been really hard."

Renni's vision blurred. He blinked quickly to clear his sight and drew a deep breath. The words lodged in his throat.

An instant later, Pia's hand was on his, gently tugging him to his feet. She stepped into his arms, wrapping hers around his torso, firm and warm, her face pressed to his chest. His arms hovered several inches away from her for a moment before he let them encircle her. Resting his cheek on the top of her head he drew a deep breath and slowly let it out.

How long had it been since he'd been hugged like this? Not since he left his father to join the training academy. So often he'd put distance between himself and anyone else that tried to get close.

"He died in that prison. Lucas stabbed him. My dad loved him like he was his own son." The words came out so soft he doubted she would hear him.

Lucas wasn't his son. And Renni's father hadn't bribed a scout for Lucas as he had for Renni.

Pia's arms tightened around him even further, letting him know she'd heard him. She didn't say anything. Sometimes, there was nothing to be said.

After another moment, he released her, and she slowly backed away.

There was nothing but kindness in her expression as she looked at him.

"So, what happens now?" He asked, his eyes holding hers.

EIGHTEEN

PIA RELEASED RENNI, STEPPING out the sphere of his warmth and scent and the steady beat of his heart.

"No one knows about this place. We sit tight for a few days. We have to give my colleagues a chance to investigate. And that's easier for them to do if they're not climbing over media every step of the way or pulling resources for protection detail. We've let it leak that you've been moved to a 'safe house' in the city."

Her heart ached for Renni. She wanted nothing more than to kiss away the grief. She understood that pit of loss. As much as she wanted to comfort him and claim him and let him know she would be there for him; she still didn't know how he felt about her panther side. She didn't know if he would accept her. All of her.

The disbelief in his face when she'd confirmed the truth had stung.

No matter that her panther had decided on him. He hadn't decided on her.

She turned to the table, collecting the empty mugs and deposited them in the sink. She turned back toward him, a comfortable distance re-established.

Whether he wanted her or not, she wouldn't leave him to deal with it alone.

She pursed her lips as she considered him across the distance of the wooden table. "When it's dark, I'll go on patrol." She watched his reaction closely, waiting for the shudder of revulsion. Instead, his expression turned curious. There were questions in his eyes.

She wanted him to ask questions, too, yet she didn't.

Have it out now while there was no going back rather than have it hang between them. She drew a breath. Or just accept that it *is* between them and focus on the job at hand. They'd had some good times in the short while since they had met. She wasn't supposed feel the way she did. He was just supposed to be a playmate.

She studied his face a little closer, recalling the moment she'd seen him cornered in the alley with a gun aimed at his chest. Defiant, even through the shock of his friend's betrayal.

The rage of his endangerment had ripped through her like nothing she'd ever experienced before. A possessive, protective instinct.

"What can I do?" He asked, bringing her back to the moment.

"Let me do my job. Stay on the property, where you can't be seen."

He moved to the arch linking the kitchen and living room, eyes scanning the space. "Small quarters."

"The deck is big enough for keepy-uppies, but if you lose your ball in the lake trying to dodge the black flies, I'm not going in after it."

"Believe it or not, I didn't think to pack a ball in my haste."

"There's one in the storage shed; if you get desperate for something to do, I can bring it in. *I could keep you occupied...*

She stopped that thought before she got herself into an uncomfortable state of need.

His eyes swept her, and she shivered.

He looked at her the same way he had right before he kissed her.

Had he heard her thoughts?

Then it was gone as he nodded. "I'm sure I can occupy myself."

This wasn't at all how Pia had imagined things would be when she thought about inviting him here. She thought they'd spend their days kayaking and swimming when they recovered from their nights of lovemaking.

Not this confined awkwardness.

This was too intimate for such suspicion between them.

As much as she didn't want to believe he was part of the planned robbery, she had to be sure. She'd told Cole and Bergeron that she would find out one way or another.

And the fact he now knew she was a shifter...

Well, they weren't supposed to be long term anyway.

A hot as hell guy on a steed of steel with flowing locks.

She brushed away the memory of their first night out, overlooking the city together.

That is where the magic had begun to bloom.

There was never supposed to be anything permanent between them.

This confinement was only for a few days.

She moved into the other half of the doorway where he stood, looked up into his face for a few seconds then descended the two steps into the living room. "The bedroom is there."

She pointed to the open door perpendicular to the front wall. "The bathroom is back through there." She gestured beyond the fireplace and sofa at the back wall where there was a small alcove. "There are two single beds in the loft that can be accessed with a drop-down ladder, I'll be sleeping on the couch."

"I don't mind taking the couch. You can have the bed."

"I can protect you better if I'm between you and the danger, Renni. That means I sleep between you and the doors."

"I'm not defenseless."

She recalled his stance when cornered. He'd been prepared to fight, despite the gun trained on him. She hadn't expected a soccer star to know how to. It was another reminder how little they knew each other.

"I'm sure under normal circumstances you can defend yourself. These aren't normal circumstances." She waited for him to process what she said.

The muscle in his jaw tightened. He clearly didn't like it, nor did he argue with her, which surprised her. Then suspicion wormed its way under her skin. She'd have to keep an eye on him.

Her eyes drank him in as she waited for him to ask any questions.

Another wave of relief flooded her, knowing he was safe. For now, at least.

During the silent drive, she'd gnawed on those feelings. She had to be careful now. There was no doubt her panther would kill to protect him. So would she, when she was honest with herself.

And she also knew what that meant to her panther.

We should be his Queen.

Her eyes were still glued to Renni's face, caressing the lines of his brow and temple, down to his set jaw. And Goddess those lips.

"Pia?" Her name was a breath as his lips parted.

She wanted nothing more than to trace her tongue along the edge of the soft lines and invite him to do the same. She shivered, recalling the feel of those lips and his tongue on her skin. Her nostrils flared as her panther inhaled his scent. Her lips parted, drawing a breath, dragging his essence back over her tongue to her throat. Taking him into her, making him even more a part of her.

This wasn't good.

She needed distance.

"There's no satellite or cable. There are a few movies in the cabinet under the TV. WIFI is spotty. I suggest you keep contact with anyone minimal." She said the first things that came to mind and moved past him to step out the front door onto the porch. Staring at the lake, she drew first one breath, then two.

This was going to be harder than she thought.

SOPHY PACED HER CRAMPED office.

Where the hell was Renni?

It was mid-afternoon and he hadn't come into the club. Was he alright? She was furious her brother had been stupid enough to attack. She blew out a breath, closing her eyes. Yes, he'd been protecting his friend from the feline trying to protect Renni from the gun in his face.

Stupid.

Why the hell was Lucas going to shoot Renni? They weren't supposed to kill anyone. Just get the trophy and get out. There hadn't been much time to talk, they'd all had to disperse and go into hiding and lick their wounds. Two of her brothers had been shot, the other seriously wounded by that goddamned cat. And Lucas now sported a cast.

Everyone could go into hiding except for Sophy.

She couldn't hide. That would look far too suspicious if she suddenly disappeared after an attempted robbery like that. She could have pled a sick day. Nerves after the trauma of night. She wasn't so sure they'd buy that, considering events had been kept extremely hushed in the ballroom, where she'd been all night.

On one hand the gala had been a success.

The robbery a complete failure.

So far, her position was still secure, if she navigated the next few days right.

There was no way they could connect her to Lucas. Or solidly connect Lucas to her brothers. They were just working as Gala serving staff.

Although, with a couple hundred attendees, anyone and everyone was a suspect.

Doubt wormed its way into her thoughts. The panther might be able to make the connections through the signature of her brothers' scents and her own.

Sophy couldn't be sure how good a feline's sense of smell was. Did the cop have enough sensory information?

Even if she did, how could she reconcile that with the local human police department. And just because her brothers might have committed a crime, didn't mean that she had too. As far as the greater world knew, Sophy lived in the city alone.

Still, the panther could possibly link her to them. No one else could.

Had she already made that connection?

Where was Renni?

She pulled her phone from her pocket, thumb hovering over his contact details.

Hey Renni, wild night last night! Just checking in to see if you're alright?

She spun at the sound of knocking on her office door, heart in her throat.

Calm yourself.

She drew several deep breaths. "Come in."

Two plain-clothed, human police officers entered, making the room feel even smaller than it was. She recognized them from the previous night once the police had arrived at the club.

"Sophy Khienak? We're detectives Hare and Maliki, leading the investigation on last night's attempted robbery." The taller one said.

She nodded. "I remember seeing you while I gave my statement. How can I help you?"

The darker haired one, the female, said, "we just have a few follow up questions. Questions not covered in the statement template, if you will."

The hairs on the back of her neck rose. "Yes of course. Would you like to sit? We can move into board room where there is more space."

"No need, this won't take long." She immediately opened with the first question, "You're new to the city, right? About a year or two?"

"Yes. A little more."

Her eyes drifted to the other officer, who bent his head to write in his note pad as his colleague asked questions.

"Alone?"

"Yes. What does this have to do with the robbery?"

"Tell us about your job here."

"I'm the personal assistant to Mr. Smith, the team manager."

"What are your duties?"

She drew a breath and listed them.

"I heard you participated in organizing the gala," the one taking the notes said, "I wasn't there, but some of my colleagues said it was a great event."

Sophy smiled. "Yes, it was, and I'm very proud to have been a small part of it."

"How lucky the event organizing team invited you to participate. Is that normal? You must be extraordinarily skilled to be able to cover two entirely different positions."

The hairs on her nape bristled further.

She shrugged, shoving away the urge to suck in more air. The room had begun to close in on her. Instead, she offered a wide, bright smile. "I guess they thought a fresh perspective would be useful. Are you sure you don't want to move into the board room? It's much more comfortable in there."

The detectives glanced at one another. The dark haired one said. "I think we're done here." The other nodded. "Thank you for your time, Ms. Khienak."

Her shoulders dropped in relief. "Any time."

"Good to know. I'm sure we'll have more questions once we make the rounds with everyone else. Long process, I'm sure you understand how thorough we have to be."

She nodded, gritting her teeth.

"We'll see ourselves out."

As soon as the door clicked shut behind them, she sucked in a deep breath.

Fuck.

Were those random questions, or did they suspect her?

They couldn't suspect her. She was too careful.

Everyone here liked her and had no reason to think she'd be involved in any kind of scheme that would endanger the club's position.

They were probably asking everyone the same sort of questions.

She nodded to herself. Drew another breath with her eyes closed.

When she opened them, she focused on her agenda.

This club isn't going to be great on its own.

She had work to do.

She'd have to contact her brothers later to ensure they were where they were supposed to be. Hidden.

Sometimes, she hated having to be the brains of everything. They couldn't be trusted to just do what was necessary without her having to guide them. She was the reason they'd been so successful in the black-market sports memorabilia business. As long as they did what she told them to, things went smoothly. They'd been successful enough to get Carlos Moreno and Lucas Gauna's attention to work the trophy job. The network was panning out.

It wasn't her fault things went sideways last night.

She'd told Lucas it was a bad idea to work the gala himself.

He'd been insistent.

And Renni Diaz had recognized him. What the hell was Lucas thinking?

Where is Renni?

She glanced down at her phone again. No response to her message.

NINETEEN

THREE DAYS.

The night air surged in and out of the screened window of the tiny cabin bedroom.

The front door creaked. It was Pia, stepping out to patrol again.

Renni lay on the bed in his boxers, staring at the ceiling, listening to the crickets.

Three days of listening to the whisper of Pia's movement through the small cabin. The click of the door as she went out to lounge on the dock. The hush of the shower water. Her sigh after her first sips of coffee. The shuffle of the couch pillows as she rolled over during sleep.

What he never heard was her panther.

The sounds of the front door as she moved through it, never the click of nails or pads of her paws walking across the forest floor under the moonlight sky. She never made a sound.

What is it like?

He tried to picture in his mind how the change happened, how he might see the world, smell it.

When the adrenalin took him while on the soccer field, he felt as though he flew from one end to the other, dodging, sliding, scanning, all while moving the ball ever forward with gentle precise taps.

What it must be like to move with absolute silence through a world of sound. To be able to jump or climb without effort.

How much power was hidden beneath her flesh?

Her flesh.

That's what he missed. The knowledge of her desire. Knowing she wanted him as much as he wanted her still.

Her presence felt like home. He wanted her at his side.

Now, with his past excavated and raw, he was sure she saw him differently.

She'd offered him comfort when he'd told her the truth. It was in her nature to do so, but he knew he'd lost her trust. And maybe her respect.

He'd never had her love.

A pang tightened his chest and gut.

His hand drifted down his bare chest to rest on his stomach.

Keeping things casual with Pia had been easy. Until her smile lit a dull room. Until she touched him. Until he was drawn into her magnetic personality. Casual had suddenly become the difficult thing.

That cute little traffic cop with the imperious scowl had a whole lot going on under the surface.

He wanted more.

He wanted Pia.

Earlier in the day, he'd asked her to cut his hair for him. Shed it like he was determined to shed his old life—for good.

"I'm about as good at cutting hair as I am at shopping," she said, dubious as he handed her the kitchen scissors.

"I trust you." He'd noticed the surprise in her expression before he turned his back to her and settled on the kitchen chair.

He waited what seemed an eternal moment before her fingers tentatively touched his scalp and the first *snicks* began. Soon, she grew bolder, her fingers threading his hair, brushing the edges of his ear and nape.

He relaxed, breathing deep of her orange and vanilla scent, her proximity and the sounds of her sighs and soft grunts of frustration as she worked, quickly became erotic as his mind drifted.

Delicious torture, until she declared she was done. His head felt lighter, both due to the shedding of the excess hair, and the lack of blood feeding his brain. It was all down between his thighs.

He thanked her, noting her concerned expression, and went to shower away the clippings and excess energy. It wasn't enough. Her closeness had him stretched thin.

Even now, hours later.

His hand drifted lower on his belly.

Her passion was unforgettable. The way she'd taken him into herself as deep as he could go. The way she'd ridden him.

His fingers curled around his hardened shaft.

He jerked, thinking about the way she bit her lip when she was close, so close to the edge. Her nails dug into his shoulders, back or ass, pulling him closer, deeper.

He wanted her. Again, and again.

He stopped.

Removing his hand from his boxers, he tucked it back behind his head as he lay staring at the ceiling, unsated.

Nothing, other than the feel of her body against his, would be enough.

Renni lay, concentrating on the cooling air after the heat of the day.

He wanted to let the peace of the place seep in. He couldn't. Not when this chasm remained between Pia and himself.

Hating confinement, he needed the open stretch of a soccer pitch to work the excess energy out of his system.

The cabin was tiny, and it was difficult not to hear one sided phone conversations, even though Pia kept her voice low. He couldn't hear much, just enough to know she was reporting to more than one superior.

The department was still investigating, as was Pia's other organization.

The Global Paranormal Security Agency, she'd called it. She was an agent, working undercover in the Montreal police department.

Not just a cute little traffic cop.

A fully trained agent. Unshakable in the tensest of situations.

Except when her apartment had been ransacked; she'd been visibly shaken after leaving her apartment.

Now, she moved as though she was in control of the world.

While there was still plenty hanging between them, having her close by felt... natural. The only discomfort came from what remained unsaid. And from the intense need to touch her again.

The idea that she probably suspected him of being involved in the robbery in some way stung. He understood it. She hadn't outright asked him, but he sensed it in the way he caught her studying him. How could anyone not be suspicious after the events of his past?

He'd alternated between gnawing on that and the vision of seeing her panther at the gala and at his home before that. And the time they'd spent together in the days before his world became skewed. Just a few days of laughing and making love. Those few memories pulled his world back the other way, almost tilting it upright again.

Nightly, she went out to patrol. Daily she stayed confined with him. Protecting him, keeping him company, or just babysitting him until her colleagues could find evidence to prosecute or dismiss him. He wasn't sure which it was, or maybe all of them.

She'd kept her distance and he'd kept his.

He'd had enough time to realize that he missed her, despite the proximity. The easy smile and laugh he'd begun to look forward to before the events following the gala had turned everything upside down, was gone.

Every night, when he slept, she invaded his dreams. The memory of their night together. The scent of her skin, the feel of her body wrapped around his. The sounds of her cries as he pleasured her.

He sighed, scrubbing his hands over his face as his body grew even more taut with desire. His mind had to reconcile that other part of her. He needed to accept that she was special in a way so different from anything he'd known before. Knowing this about her now didn't change who she was, before he was aware.

What was the problem? What was he afraid of?

He realized that he wasn't afraid of her, or what she was.

He was afraid of what it meant. Accepting something so far outside his perceived world view that it slid his paradigm out from under him, shaking his foundations.

It was real.

She was far more powerful than he could ever be. It had been a long, long time since he'd felt powerless. He'd been at the top of the world. Top of his career, his athleticism, had all the money he could ever have dreamed of as a kid, the influence he'd wanted; to do the things he wanted to see accomplished in his lifetime.

And he'd met this amazing woman who was so far above and beyond all that, making it all seem so insignificant now.

From time to time, he'd thought of what family life would be like, always shunting it aside. It wasn't for him. It wasn't something he knew how to do.

He knew soccer. That was his life. He had nothing to offer a family.

The memory of her interacting with Ella in his backyard floated back to him, and how he'd felt. His heart locked on that moment.

Renni rose from the bed, knowing he wouldn't sleep, and went out to sit on one of the couches on the front porch.

He stretched out, so that he could gaze up at the stars sprinkled across the sky over the moon-glimmered lake.

PIA PICKED HER WAY down the rocks, through the brush toward the cabin. The itch and tightness of the wounds she'd received while fighting in the alley were finally healed over. Her body had taken full advantage of the accelerated healing while being in her panther form.

Despite her concerns about being followed up into the mountains, there had been no evidence their pursuers had found them. The only scents she could detect were those of the wildlife and local inhabitants. The breeze gliding in from the lake tickled her whiskers. At the base of the steps to the porch, she stopped, head turned toward the lake, enjoying the scents drifting toward her and finally relaxed, letting down her guard.

She nearly jumped out of her fur, claws scrambling on the wooden deck when Renni's voice broke the peace of the late night.

"All's well?"

Her head whipped toward him, eyes narrowing on the crooked smile on his face. He was stretched out on the porch couch.

She huffed at him and prowled up the steps to settle between the rail and the door, deciding to keep her distance for the time being.

The moonlight lined his body in silver, creating hollows and ridges along the honed muscle of his chest and abs.

Her throat turned as dry as the driftwood littering the shoreline, as an image of sliding her tongue—her human tongue—along every one of those cliffs and valleys teased her mind. Her nostrils flared, taking in the scent of him as the lake breeze receded.

Bergamot, black pepper, and his personal scent.

He sat up and looked back at her.

"The last time I saw you like this; you were wearing the necklace I gave you. Quite the sight, you know. A powerful panther glitzed up in diamonds going tooth and claw against a hyena after stopping Lucas from putting a bullet in me. I'll never forget that."

She felt his gaze on her feline face and along her sleek coat as he regarded her thoughtfully.

"Incredible." His voice was a breath on the night air.

But.

She waited for it. Waited for him to tell her this was it. After things were settled with the hyena pack and the mob, and the investigation, they wouldn't see each other again.

Their play time was done. Finished in those brief moments in the alley behind the conference center.

Her feline half was her reality. Not his.

She'd been prepared for the end since they'd begun. And the last few days had been very quiet.

She just hadn't expected her heart to hurt so much when it was time for the words to end things.

"From the beginning we said it was just for fun. No commitment. No attachments. Keep it light and fun. No expectations. You'd go your way, I'd go mine. Fond memories." He said, eyes on hers.

Her tail curled around her front paws, the tip swaying rhythmically as she struggled to steady her heartbeat.

"Since we've been here, we've been cocooned from the world. I've never been in such a quiet, peaceful place. It encourages... reflection."

She forced her chest to draw deeper breaths as it tightened further.

"I'll be honest, Pia. That night, my paradigm was broken. I had no idea that shifters could be real, and are. I thought it was all just fiction. You've changed my world. I can't go back to a life of ignorance. It's a lot to process—having my world upended like that."

Here it comes...

She braced herself for the words to officially end it.

He drew a breath and went on.

"What has disturbed me the most is your withdrawal from me. I've always noticed the barrier—how you keep yourself separate. This is different. These last days we've been together more than ever before in this little cabin, and yet the distance between us is vast. Your secret. My past."

She blinked, unsure where this was going.

He stood, approaching, his bare feet soundless on the wooden boards.

He crouched before her, hand extended. "We need to talk."

In her panther form with her hypersensitive sense of smell, his scent was intoxicating.

Mate. Her kitty declared.

No. Pia growled back.

It took her a moment to realize he was waiting for her to shift into her human form. She stared down at his extended hand.

"Pia?"

She blinked at him. Uncertainty chased the breath out of her lungs.

Vulnerability.

The night of the attack, she'd shifted without thought, to protect him.

She didn't think she could handle his reaction if she shifted in front of him under these circumstances. Or bear the rejection. Not from *him*.

At one time, she would have told herself she didn't care. This is who she is.

Something had changed in her, even as she pushed away those ancient memories of that first time she'd been rejected by her first love.

Ridiculous.

This felt exactly like that.

That girl who'd fallen for a special boy whom she'd been so excited to share her secret with, who'd recoiled from her.

That girl was still locked somewhere in Pia's heart, to be protected, no matter how independent and powerful she'd become. Instead, she'd only shared her secret with Erin, because Erin understood. She was like Pia, but different. And something like 'shape' or 'form' didn't matter. As much as she loved Erin, they first and foremost were friends. Not destined mates.

She turned her head, peering into the dark cabin through the screen door. Her Dad's cabin.

Her dad had accepted her mother.

Even if Renni couldn't accept her, she owed it to her parents to accept herself. Which most of the time she did. Her unexpected feelings for Renni had made that old self-doubt seep to the surface.

Turning her head back to him, he still crouched, hand extended, eyes leveled on her.

Locking her eyes on his, she shifted.

Pia expected revulsion.

She hadn't expected pure wonder.

"Incredible, Pia. You're incredible."

His hand had remained outstretched, unwavering.

She dropped her gaze to it, lifting her own, tentative.

Her eyes returned to his face.

His eyes crinkled in the corners as he smiled at her.

The warmth of his hand enveloped her fingers as she slid them along his open palm. He tipped their hands up and pressed his lips to the back of her hand.

She blinked to clear the sudden blurring of her vision, before he could see any tears threatening to give away the secrets of her heart.

He helped her stand, eyes on her face, then let go of her hand so that his fingers could trace her chin.

"I'll understand if you're keeping your distance because you want to move on. I will even understand if you believe I was working for Carlos." He swallowed. "Will you let me kiss you once more before you walk away from me for good?"

"I don't believe you're working for Carlos." Her voice sounded rough to her own ears, what she could hear of it, her heart was hammering so hard. "You want to kiss me?" she couldn't stop her voice from sounding small.

"I want to do so much more than kiss you, Pia. But only if you're still interested."

He didn't think she was interested in him anymore?

She nodded as she swallowed. Processing.

She remained still as his lips descended toward hers.

They hadn't touched since that night... How many nights ago? An eternity.

The heat from his body preceded the touch of his lips, turning her veins to liquid fire.

Each time they touched, the energy between them intensified.

Mate.

No...

The latter declaration was incredibly weak.

Renni's tongue laved her lower lip and her knees buckled, sending her reeling into him, chest to chest.

His arms closed around her, supporting, as he deepened the kiss.

There was no doubt about his arousal. Hot steel pressed into her naked belly.

She broke the kiss, drawing a deep, deep breath, staring at his lips. His desire mirrored her own.

Desire.

Her heart latched onto that.

The magic of the mountain cabin brought them together once more.

"I don't know what's in store for us when we go back," he said. "I'd imagine the club will want to nullify my contract. My career is probably done. So that means I'd be free to go anywhere and do anything I please." His eyes remained on her lips as he spoke, then shot up to her eyes. "Would you like to go away with me for a while? If your colleagues don't throw me in jail as an accomplice to grand larceny?"

She blinked. A smile pulled at the corner of her lips.

"I'm finding it harder and harder to not want something more long term. The more we're together, the more I want us to be together, Pia. You're special."

The smile spread across her lips. "I'm not the only shifter, Renni."

He smiled back at her. "I know. You're special because of who you are. Your strength, determination, intelligence. Above all, your true kindness. *That's* special—*you're* special."

She could hear the increased rate of his heartbeat and sense the sincerity in his tone.

He really meant it.

"Renni, I-"

He put a gentle finger over her lips, stopping her words.

"You don't have to decide now. Think about it."

She didn't want to think about it. She already knew she wanted him.

Told you. Her kitty smirked. *Mate.*

What if down the road he changed his mind? Or if she were to lose him the way her father had lost her mother. She'd never recover from that, nor would he. Not if she went ahead with the *Mating*.

"Maybe," she whispered, not sure if her response was to Renni, or to her inner panther.

Kitty snorted in frustration.

Renni smiled. "It's a start."

Her eyes dropped to his curved lips, and she could resist no longer. Claiming him with her mouth, she pressed her naked body to his, rubbing up against him, leaving no doubt to her desire for him.

His arms came around her an instant later, hands roaming across her bare back and down to her hips and backside, squeezing and kneading before lifting her up.

Her arms went around his neck, then her legs around his waist, the heat of their bodies chasing away the cooling night air.

Renni reached for the screen door. A moment later they were in the small bedroom where he gently lay her down on the bed.

He hovered over her, staring down into her face. She drank him in equally.

Her heart swelled so that she couldn't talk, even if she'd wanted to.

She didn't.

His lips descended over hers, soft, sensual, so very tender, saying important things without words.

Returning the touches, she added her need for more. Her tongue caressed his with deliberation.

Nothing hurried or forced.

No urgency.

Finally, she pressed her palm to his chest until he stood before her. She looked up at him from her place on the corner of the bed, then slowly let her gaze travel down his throat, wide tattoo-covered shoulders, along his chest down to his bellybutton, licking her lips as her fingers trailed their way down to the waistband of his boxers. Hooking her fingers over the band, she pulled them down until they dropped to the floor.

He sprang free, extended toward her.

Leaning forward, she pressed a kiss to his stomach, then let her tongue slide along ridges of muscle. She pressed her face to his warm skin, inhaling deeply of his soap and personal scent. She pressed another kiss lower, letting the velvety steel of his arousal brush along her cheek as she moved back.

She looked up at him. His tip so very close to her mouth.

He stared down at her with hooded eyes and parted lips.

She wrapped her hand around the base of his length, holding him so he couldn't move. Maintaining eye contact, the tip of her tongue traced the head and slit, gliding along the underside and back up again.

"Fuck, Pia." He growled, his cock jerked and engorged further in her fist.

Her mouth closed around him, descending as far as she could as his fingers laced through her hair. She held him fast, controlling the speed and depth of penetration.

She took her time, savoring.

"Stop." He whispered.

With a final gentle suck, she let him pop free of her mouth and looked up into his face.

His chest rose and fell, breath shaking.

"My turn." His eyes glittered in the darkness as he lowered to a squat before her.

She kissed him, giving his tongue as much attention as she had his cock.

He broke the kiss and dropped his gaze to her belly, letting his fingers trace their way down her body, as she'd done to him, until they hovered between her thighs and slid between her slick folds and into her core. He worked her entrance, then let his thumb flick across her nub.

She gasped and bit her lip.

He looked up into her face with a grin before removing his fingers so that he could taste her.

He licked her juices from his fingers then leaned forward to plunder her mouth, mingling their tongues.

Breaking the kiss, he bent to kiss each thigh, gently urging her to hook her knee over his shoulder as he moved lower, closer.

His breath teased her flesh, causing hers to stall in her chest.

The anticipation stretched for several heartbeats.

Mercy as his lips touched her.

She groaned as his tongue laved her, moving around her nub and dipped into her channel.

She almost came in that instant.

"Jesus, Renni." Her body jerked falling back onto her elbows.

He wasn't done yet.

As she'd held him fast and devoured his length, he did the same. His hands locked her hips in place as he feasted, now plundering her sex instead of her mouth. Licking, sucking, and nibbling, until she couldn't take anymore.

"Renni! Renni stop, I'm too close." She tried to squirm away. He held tight, burying his face deeper, fucking her with his tongue so that she had no choice to give over to him. "Oh god, Renni!" her fingers clawed the edges of the mattress as her hips tilted and she gave him what he wanted.

She cried out. Dragged in a new breath and cried out again and again as he drank her release.

Her body trembled as he adorned her thighs with lingering kisses. He worked his way to her hips, along her abdomen to her breasts, paying homage to each before he returned to her lips.

"Even after a lifetime, I couldn't get enough of you." He whispered.

She was still breathing hard, but her chest froze at his soft words, bringing tears to her eyes.

She'd never have enough of him either. She knew. No matter how much she resisted, deep down she knew it. And that terrified her.

She couldn't stop the tears that escaped from the corners of her eyes before closing them.

"Hey, sweetheart, it's okay." He pressed his lips to the outer corners of her eyes, then pulled her into his lap, turning them so that his back was pressed to the bed as he sat on the carpeted floor. He held her close, when he spoke, his voice was barely a whisper. If she'd been human, the words might have sounded like another breath. "I want you for ever, Pia. If you don't want that, I'll take you as long as you'll have me. Even if that's only till morning."

Terror and joy went to war in her heart.

She leaned back so she could look at him.

His eyes glittered in the darkness as he stared back at her.

She cupped his face, pressing her lips to his.

His full erection was pressed to her bottom.

She turned around, moving until his tip was pressed to her entrance.

His eyes never left hers.

She took him in, filling her as she descended, drawing a shuddering breath.

After the release he'd just given her, she should have been sated for a week.

The feel of him hard, and pulsing deep inside, reignited the spark before it could go dormant. The pulse beat inside her, his heartbeat beneath her chest, pressed to his.

"Forever is a long time." She breathed.

His head tipped forward. "It is."

"A lifetime of this?" she rolled her hips.

He gasped, fingers gripping her thighs spread to either side of his own hips, before sliding up to grip her waist, pressing her down.

It was her turn to gasp as his tip pressed that magic spot deep inside of her, making her quiver.

"A lifetime isn't long enough."

"Forever, then," she said.

"Forever mine," he whispered against her lips as she inhaled his words before he sealed the promise with a kiss, while his hands encouraged her into motion atop him.

She writhed and ground against him, slow at first. Riding and slamming, unable to get enough, unable to get deep enough despite the fact he filled her to stretching. Until he leaned back on the bed and lifted his hips, thrusting up into her as she slammed down again and again.

She screamed as she came again.

Renni's fingers bit into her hips as he held back and flipped them so that she was on her hands and knees on the bed, panting, and he slid into her from behind. She cried out as he slammed into her, pumping until he released into her tight, spasming, channel.

She gripped him hard until his spasms dissipated.

As he slowly withdrew, his absence was sharp.

He fell onto the bed next to her, pulling her into his arms, her back pressed tight to his chest.

"Forever mine." His words drifted across her ear before he pressed a kiss just below her lobe.

Her fingers trailed over his, slipping between them, locking together so that she could pull their joined hands to her chest.

She closed her eyes and let go of the terror so that joy could occupy the space of her heart more fully.

TWENTY

RENNI'S EYES SNAPPED OPEN.

A quick glance to orient himself before he heard the sound again. A cell phone buzzed on the kitchen table. He drew in a deep breath looking down the length of his body where Pia lay curled around him deep in sleep. His chest bloomed and he smiled.

The phone buzzed again.

He kissed her forehead. "Pia."

Her head lifted at his whisper. She blinked and smiled up at him.

A frown marred her forehead when the phone's buzzing persisted.

A blink later, she'd rolled out of the bed and was out of the room before his feet had touched the thin carpet.

He grabbed a pair of boxers and followed Pia into the kitchen. She'd pulled a tee shirt on before answering her phone.

Hers then.

He picked up his phone. He had several missed calls and voice mails.

"What was their demand?"

Renni's head whipped back in Pia's direction, heart stopped.

Oh no.

Her eyes were on his face, her skin devoid of color.

He had no doubt Lucas and his crew had taken someone. The question was who? A teammate? He didn't have anyone close to him anymore. Except Pia.

They'd want money. Or the trophy, since it was the original prize, they also had to know that was an impossibility now too.

Pia ended the call after a few more exchanged words. "Captain wants us to stay here a while longer."

"Who did they take?"

Pia's lips compressed.

"Pia?"

"Ella."

The wind went out of Renni. He gripped the back of the nearest chair.

"What was the demand?"

"The trophy, ten million, and you. But that's not happening."

Lucas.

Renni straightened, "If you want her back in one piece, it's happening. We've been hiding up here long enough."

Pia studied him for an interminable moment.

"If I don't go, they *will* kill her."

She finally nodded. "I'm not handing you over to them, either. We can discuss this on the way back to the city."

TWENTY-ONE

Renni's fingers drummed his knee.

"Tell me again about Lucas. There's got to be some other way to get to him."

"We grew up together, playing football in the streets, running with the same gangs." He sighed and rubbed a hand over his face. "Until I got picked out by a scout and he didn't."

"That's when you went to a training camp."

"Yes. I didn't see him much after that except when I went home to see my father, which wasn't often. The club kept me isolated and focused on the sport. Any time Lucas and I did see each other, we argued. He accused me of thinking I was better than everyone else, too good for everyone at home. I suppose he wasn't wrong. I hated going back."

"How did the mob get involved in your life?"

Renni's hands fisted on his thighs. "After my mother died, my father's gambling increased." He snorted. "It was bad before, it got worse after she was gone. Which made it easy to believe it just never stopped." His throat tightened. "He was thoroughly submerged in Carlos's world."

"Do you think there's a chance he won't have Ella killed?"

"If he demanded I be there, and I go, I hope it's enough. I guess it depends on what else was in his demand that he really wants."

What did Carlos have planned for him, that he was expected to be part of the exchange?

Lucas had already shown his hand and pointed a gun at Renni in that alley. Heat of the moment? Or his own agenda?

He had no idea how far he would go. Lucas was more of a wild card, where Carlos saw himself as a businessman. He dealt with transactions.

Renni's gut was telling him that Ella was in more danger than he was willing to let on to Pia.

Telling her there was a chance Ella could come away alive if he participated was the only way he could persuade her to let him be involved.

He glanced at her profile as she concentrated on the road before them.

"I seriously doubt my bosses are going to let you put yourself in danger," she said as though reading his thoughts.

He'd figured that would be the case.

He'd have to think of a way to get to Lucas.

He had to. He couldn't let Ella get hurt because of Renni's choices in the past.

Besides, Renni had an agenda of his own now. Lucas was the man that put a shank in his father.

"My dad died in prison because I refused to do what Carlos wanted. It's my fault he's dead. I was naïve to think my dad wouldn't become expendable to Carlos. They'd been friends for so long—before Carlos became the powerhouse that he is."

"No, Renni, it isn't your fault. He made his own choices. And he died because someone decided to kill him. Not you. It's not your fault."

"I could have prevented it."

"We both know that's how these guys work. They suck you in, drown you, let you breathe a little, then drown you some more until you're thankful they let you have that little gasp of air. It never ends."

Of course, he knew she was right. It didn't abate the deep sense of guilt that'd been gnawing at him since his father's incarceration, and especially since his death.

"Opportunists are always going to find new ways to get what they want at the expense of others. Especially of the vulnerable. I've seen it time and again in my line of work."

Renni was compelled to save Ella. An innocent, dragged into his world simply because she had the misfortune to live next door to him.

He'd never forgotten the brutality of street life in his home city. Never forgot the feel of his fist breaking flesh and bone in a brawl. The savage intimacy of your body connecting to your opponent's in the heat of rage, or fear, or simple brute aggression.

His hands itched for that brutal impact now, because if anything happened to Ella, he no longer had any reservations about breaking the face of the man that harmed her—an innocent child.

Old friend or not.

TWENTY-TWO

"THE EXCHANGE IS TO take place at the Mont Royal Observatory viewing terrace. They say they'll have Ella. They let me speak very briefly to her; she's scared, but unharmed," Captain Bergeron said.

Renni drew a breath. Relief didn't settle in. She wasn't out of danger.

"And all they want is Renni and the trophy?" Pia said.

Captain Bergeron nodded. "And ten million dollars."

"Of course." Renni muttered.

"The World Association doesn't want to let the Global Cup be used in a hostage situation like this. They said it's supposed to represent global unity of sport. And unity, or any such symbol, shouldn't be bartered. They won't deal with kidnappers and terrorists."

"Not even for the life of a child?" Pia straightened and paced across the room.

"It's a symbol. That's the whole point of any trophy. The fact that it's made of gold is secondary."

"If Carlos is given what he wants, there's a chance she'll be released unharmed. A chance. He's allowed it in the past. Not always."

"Unpredictability. If there's a hope we can get the kidnap victim back, we'll deal. If there isn't, no deal at all." The Captain muttered.

"I *will* go in for the exchange with the money." Renni said to Bergeron.

"No." Pia said.

"You have no training." The captain said.

Pia stepped in front of Renni. "I won't let you do anything so risky. Lucas was going to put a bullet in you in that alley."

"I'm not going to let him hurt an innocent child just to protect myself."

"It's stupid, Renni. It's not happening."

"I will go, Pia. I can't not."

"You can't if we put you in a holding cell," she said.

Voice hard, Bergeron said, "aside from the fact that this is your life we're talking about—and Ella's too—you aren't trained. Having the trophy involved ensured that the world's eyes are going to be on us. If this goes badly and we lose Ella and/or you, this looks bad not just for the precinct, but the city, and probably our country, too."

"Everything is about image in this world, isn't it?" Pia snarled.

"What time is the exchange?" Renni asked.

"After dark tonight."

"*Dios*, that's not much time, is it?"

"They aren't screwing around. We tried to buy a few extra days, they wouldn't take it."

"Who can get any bank to release that kind of money in one day?" Renni scrubbed his hands over his face as images of Ella rolled through his mind. If they harmed her, he would rip Lucas apart himself. It seemed that no matter how hard he tried to leave the ruthlessness of the streets, they had a way of hooking their tentacles on and reeling him back in. And Lucas was that hook. It was always Lucas dragging him back, no matter how far he managed to go.

"I'll call my squad lead and see who's close by," Pia said, sliding her hand over Renni's shoulder. "We'll find a way to save Ella. It's what we do." Her voice was soft.

Renni was making plans of his own.

"COLE HERE. WHAT'S UP, Jensen?"

Pia blew out a breath. "I had Renni Diaz in protective custody. Now we've got a kidnapping. Human child. Humans and the pack of hyena shifters I reported before. Call came in this morning, meeting is tonight."

"Shit. Looks like they decided to draw you out. The rest of the squad is spread out. Let me talk to agents Maeda and Kane to see who I can call in." Cole's voice softened. "Pia, just remember you're not alone. The whole of the GPSA is a team, not just your unit."

Pia drew in a deep breath and let it ease out. "I know. Thanks, Cole," she said.

She had to keep reminding herself that since signing up, she was part of a larger entity. She'd been so used to working alone, she'd only just become used to relying on her team. Even though she would have faced off against the hyenas on her own if she had to, she couldn't deny the relief knowing Cole was going to find her some back up. She just prayed that whoever came, would get there in time.

She replaced the phone in her pocket and looked up at Bergeron with a nod, then glanced through the glass dividing Bergeron's office from the one next to it, where Renni paced while talking on his phone.

With her sensitive hearing, she could hear his elevated voice negotiating to have funds released. She swallowed hard. He was doing all that he could to ensure Ella's safe release.

Pia's shoulders sagged with relief, knowing that her gut had been right about Renni. That despite her brain's suspicions of his involvement, that he was as innocent as she'd hoped.

"Make sure he stays here when we go."

Captain Bergeron's eyebrows shot up. "Oh, he's made it very clear that he's going to be there one way or the other, Pia. He's supposed to be part of the exchange. Don't worry, we'll make sure he's equipped."

"I can't believe you've changed your mind and are letting him get involved." She spun toward the captain, snarling.

His eyes widened a fraction before his expression slammed into a scowl. "Constable, stand down. Your friend over there made the compelling argument that he knows this guy, that he has a chance to get through to him."

"Yeah, the last time they had an encounter that guy had a gun aimed at Renni and actually pulled the trigger. He will know that Renni won't be there alone." Her eyes continued to follow Renni beyond the glass window as he paced the length of the neighboring room.

"Pia, his priority is that child."

"I know," she said, "So is mine." She couldn't stop the tightness that had clamped a fist around her gut now when she looked at him. She wasn't a psychic, but her gut told her plenty. And right now, she knew this wasn't going to go as smoothly as they all hoped.

"THIS WASN'T PART OF the agreement."

Lucas Gauna looked up from the emails on his screen as Sophy Khienak stomped into the room. "And?"

"And? I was very clear when we took this job, we do item extractions. No one gets hurt. No one dies. And that also means we don't kidnap people."

"It's just one kid. What's the big deal? Besides, Carlos Moreno isn't happy about not having the item."

"Are you willing to go back to jail? Kidnapping and murder sentences are much higher than burglary and robbery. You couldn't have forgotten already?"

He shrugged. "I have no intention of getting caught."

"No one ever does." She sneered, tossing her hair over her shoulder. "My brothers are only just healed from your alley fiasco. What were you thinking? *No one* was supposed to get hurt. And now you've taken some kid?"

He closed the laptop, stood, and sauntered toward Sophy.

She stiffened, head tipped back, eyes downcast on his hands. A woman used to an unpredictable heavy hand.

Was she afraid of him? Interesting. He hadn't expected someone like... like *her* to be wary of him—a human. He supposed he had a reputation.

"Don't be nervous." He said reaching for her.

"I'm not nervous." She snapped, still leaning away as his hand drifted toward her hair.

"We had a good time last week."

Her chin shot up higher. "That was last week."

"And a marvelous week it was, wasn't it?" He grinned, remembering the sensation of those luscious lips of hers.

She shrugged. "Sure."

He frowned.

"This week can be even better if you're a good girl."

She glanced up at his face, the tip of her tongue slipping over her lip.

Yes, she certainly was wild for him, there was no doubt.

Her body eased toward him, toward his promise.

A woman after his own heart. She liked it as rough as he did. So long as he promised sexual gratification in the end, she let him do anything he wanted to her.

She was such an animal.

And he held her leash, which held the leashes of her brothers—her pack.

What a surprise it had been to discover this talented little gang of thieves working the black-market circuit in Montreal were shifters—Hyena shifters at that. He never in his wildest dreams could have imagined such a scenario.

It would be easy for her to kill him. A thrill of the power he had over her shot through him.

His fingers curled around her nape dragging her against him. She gasped, lips parting.

"None of this was part of the agreement either, Sophy." He ground their hips together. "Consider what I can do to you a personal perk. A favor. You can return the favor."

She smiled, allowing her extended canine teeth to show. "A favor, is it?"

Lucas didn't flinch away from the threat. Like when dealing with the heavy weights in prison, he powered on, everything hinged on the weakness in her which he'd hooked his fingers into; he pressed harder.

Aware of her heightened senses, he leaned forward a fraction and breathed, "I'm aware of your desperation. Your emptiness. That gaping emptiness that I'm able to fill. It's so easy for me to make you scream, Sophy. And once the job is done, we're done too."

The sound of her growling sent shivers up his arms.

His free hand shot toward her crotch, grabbing tight. "You give me what I want, I'll give you want you want."

Fuck, he loved the power he had over her. He was definitely going to buy her a collar.

"My brothers won't like it, Lucas. I can't guarantee they'll participate. Besides, how do you know Renni will cooperate? And what about the cop he's been fucking?"

He gripped her harder, but eased his hand so that the pressure was a combination of pain and pleasure.

"Renni knows I don't fuck around."

His fingers applied further pressure, making her gasp. He grinned when her eyes glazed over. Her extended teeth receded as she licked her lips.

"She's a shifter. If she cares about him, she will protect him."

"Then it's up to you to ensure she's kept busy, and he's left to me. Simple."

He pressed his lips to hers as his fingers continued to alternate between massaging and deep kneading.

"And the cops?" Her voice was tight.

Her arousal was heightening.

"Don't worry about them, Sophy. You and your brothers focus on taking out the shifter. I can take care of the rest. I have plenty of men."

"Lucas..." her eyes were glazed as she looked up into his face.

He pressed a chaste kiss to her cheek, releasing her. "That favor, Sophy," he whispered, and eased back to look down at her, keeping his expression impassive.

Disappointment fluttered across her face. She swallowed, nodding, before turning her disappointment away from him, and she schooled her expression before leaving the room.

She was so fucking vulnerable to him.

Once she was gone, he turned and poured himself a drink before returning to the task he'd been occupied with before her interruption—securing the extra men he'd just mentioned.

TWENTY-THREE

PIA PROWLED THROUGH THE shadows on silent paws.

She'd left a cache with her uniform, vest, and weapons well hidden in the cemetery adjacent to the viewing terrace where the meeting was to take place. She had a small pouch looped around her neck.

Local officers were stationed at various points around the mountain top, including Hare and Maliki, close to the drop point at the viewing terrace. There was an incredible amount of greenery for Lucas' men to hide in, which that also meant there were plenty of hiding places for the department to take position in too.

While Pia was scouting potential enemy locations, her primary objective was to find Ella and get her to safety.

Bits of bark cracked under her claws as she pulled herself up a great maple trunk. Settling on a sturdy overhanging branch, she shifted into her human form.

Crouching on bare feet, back pressed to the trunk for balance, she opened the small pouch slung from her neck, withdrawing the tiny earpiece to put it in place.

"Check in." She kept her voice low in case there were other shifters with keen hearing also scouting the grounds that she couldn't scent.

"Copy. Lirikai and I are positioned in the trees below the terrace." Agent Carson Perenga said.

"I could kiss the two of you for coming on such short notice, Carson."

Carson's chuckle vibrated in her ear. "Anytime, Pia. We were still in the area on vacation. Besides, I owed you one after the incident at the Port."

"How's the human trafficking case going?"

"We gained a lot of intel from those involved in this latest take down thanks to your help patching us in with the local police department. We're really close to cracking the center, I can feel it," Carson said.

"That's what I'm here for—it's a welcome diversion from the monotony of speeding tickets and seatbelt checks."

"Likewise." Carson said.

Pia eyed the pathways again. "You're a good catch, right?"

"I played ball as a kid."

"Can you catch hundred-pound cats?"

"If I have to."

"Options may be limited. Be ready."

"Yes ma'am."

Captain Bergeron's voice broke in. "Vehicles approaching."

"I smell corruption. They're almost here." Lirikai's voice chimed in.

"Renni, are you ready?"

"Ready," he said, voice firm through the earpiece.

"All units are in position. We have eyes on the suspects." Bergeron confirmed, the sound of his walkie crackled through the smaller network of the earpieces.

"Copy. I'm going dark now." Pia secured the earpiece back in the pouch and listened. The crunch of gravel signaled approaching cars.

They expected the hyena shifters to come, but couldn't be sure that they were the only paranormals among the crew.

She closed her eyes and drew a deep breath, shifting on the exhale.

ELLA WAS IN DANGER because of him. An innocent child.

Renni sank his hands into his pockets to alleviate the gnawing worry.

Pacing the length of the viewing platform's thick balustrade, he peered down the substantial drop to the tops of maple, oak and birch in full summer foliage. He couldn't see the agents that had come in to help Pia. He drew a deep breath of the sweet humid air, rich with the greenery of the mountain top park.

He looked back across the skyline for the hundredth time, memories of his recent visit here with Pia invaded his thoughts.

A brave deed.

He scowled, turned, and paced back as he waited for Lucas to show.

He was sick and tired of this invisible line that kept him tethered to Lucas and Carlos and that old world that he'd been trying to leave for most of his life now.

He resisted the urge to pull at the extra layers under his clothes, trapping the heat and making his skin itch. He glanced again at the small bright pink jacket he'd placed on the balustrade for Ella. Below it lay the black canvas bag of money on the stone terrace by his feet.

It wasn't easy pulling in that much money. His teammates and the greater athletic community had come through for him—for Ella.

Maybe a single person or entity couldn't withdraw a single large sum like ten million dollars, but multiple sources could pull smaller amounts.

The first person he had called was Rosa, the club's internal powerhouse when it came to bringing people together. Then the club's manager, Daniel Smith, who had surprised Renni by enthusiastically promising to reach out to the Board and the city's other clubs. His agent, Brian Gerrard, had also promised to make some phone calls.

Everyone had come on board, the whole damned club. Even some of the investors. And they were all clear on the possibility of never seeing the sums returned if things went sideways. All those community charity events, time spent mingling, had just paid off. Many of these people had children of their own, or special nieces and nephews. They were all committed to try.

If this wasn't a show of community unity, he didn't know what was.

Again he turned back to the glimmer of city lights spread out before him, beyond the balustrade.

He drew a deep breath to dispel the emotion that had begun to lodge in his throat.

He had no illusions that Lucas could kill him this night—if that was what he wanted.

Somewhere along the way, Lucas' work had dipped him in blood, and now his attention was set on Renni. He understood now that this rivalry that had grown between himself and Lucas was combustible. Lucas' deep-seated jealousy meant he was out to destroy Renni. Had Carlos agreed to this? It didn't matter, it wouldn't change anything. Lucas would do as he pleased.

Renni wasn't going to make it easy for him. His focus was exclusively on ensuring Ella's safety, above all else.

He ran a hand through his clipped hair. The rosary wrapped around his wrist drew his attention and he pressed his lips to the crucifix out of habit. And for Ella.

He glanced down into the treetops far below him again. He had no idea how anyone way down there could help them way the hell up here.

He had to trust that Pia knew what she was doing.

She said that the hyenas probably wouldn't shift unless they had to. She'd also told him that, in her world, to expect the unexpected.

Captain Bergeron had ordered the park's security surveillance system turned off for the evening in a bid to make things easier for Pia's colleagues to do whatever they would have to do if things got complicated.

Perspiration now coated his skin under the layers he wore. He was sure the tee shirt between his skin and the vest was soaked through, as were his calves beneath his jeans. He didn't care how ridiculous the idea was, he'd worn his shin guards. If there was a fight, he'd be all in.

He turned as a vehicle approached the chalet set between the woods and the platform. Several more vehicles trailed behind the first. They all parked out of his line of sight, behind the building.

His mind raced, dragging his pulse with it.

This was it.

He squared his shoulders and waited.

Car doors slammed. A moment later clusters of men strode toward him from either side of the chalet.

A few of the faces were familiar. A couple he'd seen the night of the gala working as wait staff. His chest tightened, recognizing a few more faces from his distant past. He dropped his gaze, seeking the face that mattered.

Ella.

The men fanned out creating a wall, blocking the two paths and exit routes from the vast viewing terrace.

Renni rolled his shoulders, preparing for the coming confrontation, then forced his body to relax, breathing deep.

Captain Bergeron's whisper in his ear nearly made him jump out of his skin. He'd forgotten about the earpiece that connected him to Captain Bergeron, Pia, and her colleagues, in those few seconds.

"The child is here."

Renni's heart hammered. He breathed deep again.

He stood alone, nowhere to go. Exposed and vulnerable.

Lucas or one of the other men could just shoot him, take the bag of money and drive off.

A couple of the men stepped aside to allow space for Lucas and Ella to breach their wall.

"Renni!" Ella's high voice carried across the terrace.

Lucas jerked her arm to silence her.

Renni stepped forward, then stopped himself. He needed to stay where he was.

Ella needed him to hold his ground.

He crouched, letting his wrists rest on his knees. Nonthreatening.

"Renni Diaz," Lucas said, cocking his head, his voice a lazy challenge. "The great footballer. International superstar, whose star has fallen. Crashed and burned."

Lucas' right forearm sported a brace, reminding Renni of the injury Pia had inflicted on him during the fight in the alley.

Ella tried to pull her arm from Lucas' grasp, scowling hard enough there was no doubt she disliked the man.

Lucas' hand snapped open.

She stumbled, struggling to maintain her balance. With a quick glance at Lucas, she ran straight for Renni, launching herself into the safety of his arms which he immediately closed around her.

"I've got you, *cara*." He whispered.

"Child released." Bergeron's whisper crackled in his ear, acknowledging to the others that he had her.

He rubbed his hands over her bare arms. "Here, I've brought you a jacket." He said as he reached toward the bright pink coat draped over the balustrade.

"But I'm not-"

"*Shhh*, that's alright. We don't want you to catch a chill before we get you back to your parents," he said, quickly cutting off her protest. He stood, snapped the jacket open, giving it hard shake over the edge of the balustrade before bringing it down around Ella's shoulders. "Perenga, whatever you're doing down there, I hope you're ready." He muttered.

"Huh?" Ella said.

"Do you like kitties, Ella?"

Her head bobbled up and down as he slid the zipper up to meet her chin.

Cracking, snapping and rustling sounded from among the trees far below them, followed by a rumbling growl. The hair stood up on his arms and nape.

"Is the trophy in that bag too, Diaz?"

Renni turned back to Lucas. "You knew the trophy would be a long shot. The money is there."

"I told you to bring the money *and* the trophy, Renni. That was the deal."

"You've got me and the money. That's enough."

Lucas' jaw dropped, then rounded in a grin. "You always were an arrogant prick."

"Got me places, didn't it?"

"It's also going to get you hurt," Lucas said, pulling a gun from within his jacket with his left hand and pointed it at Renni, just like he had in the alley.

Renni understood; he was just looking for an excuse to shoot him. And not fulfilling the impossible demand was the perfect excuse.

Movement caught his eye to his far left. The dull streetlamp flashed in Pia's eyes as she prowled through the shadows behind the wall of men blocking the paved path between the end of the balustrade and the chalet.

Renni crouched down to Ella's height again and whispered, "Close your eyes tight and keep them closed no matter what. Understand?"

Her brows rose in concern. She nodded her head as she squeezed her eyes shut like he told her to.

"Never mind the kid, Renni, you have bigger problems," Lucas snapped.

Renni gently pushed her closer to the stone balustrade and stood so that she was behind him, hidden from view. He faced Lucas.

"Where's your sidekick, Lucas? Your personal assistant?"

Sophy wasn't anywhere to be seen. Were her brothers among Lucas' men?

"I don't know what you're talking about," he said, brow lifted, smirking.

He had to ensure Lucas' attention was on him and not Ella. He bent, reaching for the canvas bag, tossing it toward Lucas, in the opposite direction from where he'd seen Pia's shimmering eyes. "It's all there. The ten million. Cash." He emphasized.

Lucas waved one of his goons over to grab the bag. "Check it." The gun lowered.

The goon jogged over, grabbed the bag and brought it over to Lucas, unzipped it and tilted it open so that the lamp light shone into it. "Looks like it's all there, boss."

"It's all in fucking Canadian bills, Renni." Lucas snarled, head whipping back in his direction. "You may as well have just given me half of the ransom demand and spat in my face, you arrogant, arrogant, fucker!"

Renni didn't miss the look of confusion as the goon peered at the bills again. "What's wrong with it, boss?"

"American dollars, Renni." He said yanking the zipper closed again, hiding the offensive colorful bills.

Renni shrugged holding up his hands. "The ransom demand wasn't as specific on currency as it was on the trophy or delivery person. Nor did you give us much time." He shrugged, bracing his feet, ensuring his body still shielded Ella.

"Take him. And take the kid too." Lucas snarled at his men, raising the gun again. "I'm going to enjoy breaking your arrogant face."

A silent black blur charged out of the bushes with a great leap and streaked along the top of the stone balustrade toward Renni. By the time anyone noticed Pia's movement, she was already adjacent to Renni's position.

With his attention on Lucas, Renni saw when Lucas gripped the handle of the gun to cock it, aim following Pia's path along the edge of the terrace look-out. Renni moved to block Lucas' line of sight as a crack resounded through the air.

He was keenly aware of Ella's scream.

As he was slammed back into the stone rail, he glimpsed Pia's jaws locking on the back of Ella's bright pink jacket by the scruff. She launched herself over the edge into nothingness, disappearing from his view in a blink.

Renni's ears rang, pain thundered through his torso where the bullet had struck the hidden Kevlar vest, lungs devoid of air as he stared up at the stars hanging over the mountain top.

TWENTY-FOUR

HE DIMLY REMINDED HIMSELF he wasn't going to die, though in the eternal seconds he spent waiting for his lungs to drag air back into them, he felt like he wanted to.

Christ, he was going to hurt tomorrow. If he survived the rest of the night.

In his ear, Bergeron issued rapid fire orders, sending the police in as soon as the agent called Lirikai confirmed that Ella was safe.

Renni struggled to his feet as a giant, clawed hand appeared over the edge of the terrace.

"What the fuck is that?" someone shouted.

Pia jumped off the appendage and approached him, sniffing. His ribs ached, but he was breathing again.

Lucas was backing away, gun still extended in Renni's direction. Several hyenas ran into view, seemingly to engage Pia. They skittered on the flagstones on seeing the claws curled around the balustrade.

If the situation wasn't so dire, Renni would have laughed at the widened eyes of the beasts as their paws scrambled. Some of the goons had turned and were firing at the police officers encircling the woods surrounding the chalet.

Bag of money still clutched in his fist; Lucas fired at the claw before he turned to run away from the scaly beast that had climbed up the side of the mountain.

Pia gave chase to the hyenas.

Renni, breathing again, got to his feet and stumbled after Lucas, shaking off the shock of being shot.

Years of hard training for speed and endurance gave him the edge he needed as he sprinted, then turned his body so that he slid—never his career had he ever done so—two footed into Lucas' legs, bringing him down in a hard and dirty tackle. The distinctive sound of bone crunched. Renni winced, but didn't stop. Lucas struggled to get back to his feet, despite the hard injury, glancing off to where the money bag had rolled.

Lucas turned his gun in Renni's direction again. This time, Renni swung his foot toward the weapon as though it were an air-born soccer ball, booting it so hard it flew up onto the roof of the chalet in the distance.

Weaponless, Lucas stared in shock at his hand, sporting a few more breaks from the impact of Renni's foot. He stumbled back a few paces, bringing up his fists to defend himself. Despite the breaks, he tried to curl his hand into a fist, the other hand also weak from the injury supported by the brace.

In the depth of the woods, snarls and yips filled the night air in one direction as shouts and the exchange of gunfire came from the other.

"Turn yourself in, Lucas."

"Fuck you, Renni."

Renni shrugged. "Suit yourself, Lucas. You're done kidnapping children and blackmailing old men."

"Your father?"

Renni nodded.

"I was done with that when I got bored with the whole matter and shanked him. It was time to move onto bigger things."

"Carlos *didn't* order it?"

"Carlos? Nah, I lied about him giving the kill order. He came to the prison to tell me he was going into retirement when I got out and he was getting things organized for my take over. He hinted he wouldn't be too sad, should I choose to cut any dead weight. So, I chose."

"*All* of this, is your doing? My father loved you, Lucas."

"Your father was nothing to me. Carlos replaced him as my mentor when he told me how your father had betrayed me by getting you off the streets, leaving me to rot." Lucas shrugged. "I just really wanted to break your legs, Renni. From the time the scouts raised you up and out of the neighborhood, filled your head with crap, made you think you were better than all of us. I just really wanted to break your fucking legs so I wouldn't have to turn on the television and see your fucking face all over it, all the damned time."

"Why? Because it should have been you, Lucas?"

"Yeah. It should have been me."

"Don't you think it would have been, if you were good enough?" Renni snarled, taking another step toward him, taunting. "You killed my father because of your petty jealousy." He continued advancing toward his childhood friend. In his long career, no matter the hits he'd taken on the field, Renni had never, ever, retaliated with violence. In this moment, he wasn't on a sports field. This was the desperate violence of the streets pushing a lifetime of suppressed rage to burn up through his heart.

He'd never, ever wanted to commit as much violence on anyone as he did this moment on his old friend.

No, they'd ceased being friends the moment the scouts had come to their neighborhood.

Lucas had made sure of that.

Despite his injuries, Lucas came at Renni, bolstered by his decades of jealousy-fueled rage. The adrenaline likely masking the pain of the fractures in Lucas' leg and fingers.

It had been many years since Renni had been in a brawl. Some things the body has muscle memory for. And his reflexes were still very sharp.

He dodged Lucas' swings. Off-balance, Lucas stumbled. Renni's quick grasp took hold of Lucas' shirt front, holding him in place as he let his fist crack into his face.

The fury blocked everything else but the feel of driving his fist into Lucas' face, a second and third time. Bone crunched, flesh split, blood splattered.

As he pulled back his fist for the fourth strike, something large and solid collided into him, sending him sprawling several yards away from Lucas.

A hyena snarled in his face.

In the next moment, it was sent careening, much like Renni had been.

His head snapped toward the sounds of feline growling as Pia and the hyena wrestled for dominance, jaws snapping at each other.

Lucas lay on the grass, chest heaving, face up to the sky.

The adrenaline must be wearing off.

Renni got to his feet, flexing his damaged hand, watching the powerful beasts try to maul one another, both injured.

He didn't know what to do to help Pia, and he doubted she'd want him to interfere.

A few seconds later the hyena went still, pinned to the ground with Pia's jaws locked on the vulnerable underside of its throat. Both animals remained motionless except for their heaving sides.

Was the hyena giving in or biding its time?

Another moment later and it didn't matter. Police officers approached; guns trained on Lucas and the beasts. He recognized detectives

Hare and Maliki approaching, taking post on either side as two more officers secured Lucas, leading him away.

"Don't shoot the panther." Renni called, drawing Maliki's attention. On seeing him, Maliki nodded before returning her attention back to the animals.

"I don't know what the hell is going on here," Hare said, "Or where the hell that dragon-thing came from, but this is one fucked up night."

Renni realized he must have lost the earpiece at some point. "Ella—she's alright?"

"She's with Captain Bergeron and her parents." Maliki confirmed.

Renni's entire body sagged. Even though they'd reported she'd made it to agents Perenga and Lirikai safely, he had known he wouldn't be relieved until she was with her family.

As though called by Renni's thoughts, Agent Carson Perenga emerged from the woods carrying two black bags, one of which was the money bag. From the other, he extracted plain black sweats.

"Officers, we can take it from here."

"But-" Hare sputtered, looking down at the wild animals.

"It's alright, we can handle this."

Captain Bergeron approached from a path leading up to the grounds where they stood behind the chalet.

"It's alright."

"We don't have an animal control unit here yet," Maliki said, wide eyed.

"No need."

Pia gave a growl that was muffled by the hyena's throat. Maliki and Hare's eyes widened, neither lowered their weapons.

The hyena responded with a whine, ending in a huff.

Pia released her opponent, took several steps toward Perenga, her snout reaching for the clothing.

The two detectives stared dumbstruck as the panther ran off toward the bushes with the clothes.

The hyena rolled to its feet, remaining where it was.

Pia approached barefoot, dressed in the black sweats from the direction of the bushes and retrieved the extra set of clothes from agent Perenga, throwing them to the ground in front of the hyena.

"Come on, Sophy."

"Officer Hare, shall we have a brief chat?" agent Perenga said, drawing the man away. Renni turned to join them, while officer Maliki remained with Pia to ensure Sophy cooperated.

"Holy shit!" Maliki yelped, "In my entire career, I have never seen anything like that."

Hare jerked to turn around and see what they were talking about.

Renni held him fast. "Just give them a moment."

Lirikai approached from the other direction. "The rest of the hyena pack is secure," she said to Carson and Renni.

"Hyena pack?" Hare stared from Lirikai to Renni.

"Detective, in the line of duty sometimes you're going to experience things that are pretty far out of the ordinary. Tonight is one of those experiences. You just have to learn to roll with it," Agent Carson Perenga said.

Hare snorted. "More like over-worked, stressed-induced, hallucinations."

"Sometimes." Perenga allowed.

"Like, I thought I saw a dragon climb over the edge of the terrace earlier."

"Oh, you did." Lirikai smiled, tossing Carson a wink.

"I have to say, you handled that very well," Perenga said, patting Hare's chest in a friendly matter with claws extended. "Very professional. Great training."

"I'll buy the department a round of drinks at the pub later." Renni offered. "You've earned it after this."

TWENTY-FIVE

THE LOCAL OFF-DUTY OFFICERS filled the *Chatton Noir* so that they spilled out onto the sidewalk outside the old stone building, celebrating their big success.

They greeted Pia and Renni with cheers and congratulations as they made their way to the door and inside to the bar.

"Complements of the captain," the bartender said, placing their sweating drinks on the aged wood in front of them. "Table in the back room," she added, with a nod in that direction.

"Thanks," Pia smiled, picked up their drinks, and handed the club soda to Renni.

"I'm picking up a round for everyone here, including you," Renni said to the bartender, who acknowledged with a smile.

Pia led the way, Renni following close behind. The going was slow, for such a short distance; it seemed everyone was determined to say a few words to both of them as they made their way.

In the far corner, set apart from other tables, Captain Bergeron sat with Detectives Hare and Maliki. Agents Carson Perenga and Lirikai were with them.

"Thanks for the drinks," Pia said, saluting the captain and greeting everyone present.

"Here's to saving the kid and catching the criminals," Carson said, standing with his drink.

Everyone else did likewise, repeating his words and clinking glasses.

They all sipped their drinks and reclaimed their seats so they could talk.

Pia looked at each of the faces around her.

This, right here, is what she was meant to do. Bridge the gap between GPSA and cross-border human partners.

For almost a year, she'd been alone, with only the captain and Erin knowing the smallest bits of information about her and who she was. Her true identity had still been a secret. Now the captain was becoming much more aware of what her world was really like, as were Hare and Maliki. That was enough. Maybe they should have let them in on her secret earlier—prepared them for this hidden world of shifters sooner. It just hadn't been her call to make.

Knowing when and how to reveal the paranormal world to the mundane one is a fragile operation.

"My position with the department is almost at its end. Another month or two and I'll be reassigned," Pia said, drawing everyone's attention.

"Our department heads are securing Pia's replacement. Someone that is originally from the area and can be more permanent. They've been out on assignment for a long time and are ready to come home," Captain Bergeron said, taking a sip from his drink. "I look forward to meeting the newcomer, but I'll be sorry to see Constable Jensen go. She's been such a valuable asset to the department."

"You're not getting rid of me completely. I still have my dad's cabin in the mountains, where I intend to spend a great deal of time when I'm not on duty."

"And surely, attending as many local games as you can." Maliki winked at Pia and grinned at Renni.

Pia's chest tightened as she smiled back at Maliki. Her glance at Renni was less certain. He was studying her face.

"Are you going to make me wait for the final report, or are you going to explain how we ended up with hyenas in our park?" Hare demanded, his normally soft voice much louder than usual.

Pia chuckled as she turned her attention back to his flushed, incredulous face. She picked up her drink, took a sip, and considered her explanation. "Thanks to the work you and Maliki did on the robbery ring, I was able to go back and pick up clues that would have been impossible for a non-paranormal to find, all leading back to the hyenas. Their paw prints and scents and enhanced abilities to move undetected. Sophy used her position at the club to mark certain people of distinction and relay the information to her pack, who organized the robberies using human thieves." She looked up at Hare's owlish expression and Maliki's frown of disbelief, continuing. "They were incredibly skilled at what they did; without being able to connect them to the robberies as shifters, they might never have been caught. They did all the leg work and hired humans to collect the wares. With the human buffer, it kept them in the clear. They made a lot of money on the black market from the collections they pilfered." Pia said.

"Using those black-market connections, Lucas hired them to work the trophy job and to get to me." Renni sipped his drink.

"Seems to me it was a risky job to take on, for a crew that had been so successful in their dealings," Hare said.

Pia shrugged. "Who knows what Sophy's motives were?"

"She's a full-on narcissist, as is Lucas. So... just believing she could do it, and get away with it, was probably enough." Renni said.

Maliki nodded. "See it time and again." She shrugged and smiled. "Keeps me employed."

Renni finished the last of his club soda and set it on the table next to Pia's near-empty drink and leaned close. "Want to go for a ride?"

The timbre of his voice sent a swirl of shivers up her nape.

She grinned. "Of course." She slid her hand along his thigh.

They stood and said their goodbyes.

"Hang on, we'll follow you out," Carson said, grabbing his jacket. He and Lirikai said their goodbyes to the Captain, Maliki and Hare. It was just as slow going on the way out, with the celebration level heightened.

Out on the sidewalk, Pia drew a deep, cleansing breath, free of alcohol fumes, laughing. "I haven't seen this place that lively in all the months I've been here."

"Cracking a major case like this one gives a good cause to celebrate." Lirikai smiled.

"We won't keep you from your ride," Carson said with a grin, "I just wanted to let you know that Lirikai and I are heading out in the morning. Cole said she'll touch base with you Monday. She wants you to take the rest of the week off—Maeda's orders. It's been cleared with Bergeron."

He offered Pia a hand. She shook it, then Lirikai's.

He went on. "You did good work here, Agent Jensen."

"What's happening with them all?" Renni asked.

"Sophy and her pack have been taken into GPSA custody. Lucas and his human accomplices will go through the usual judicial system." Lirikai said. "He's not going to see freedom for a long time."

"He had a record back home; now, adding everything he did here, plus kidnapping?" Renni shook his head.

"And he confessed to killing your father in prison, Renni," Carson said, "We all heard it through your earpiece."

Renni straightened, turning his gaze to Pia, grief clouding his expression.

"Thanks again for having our backs," Pia said to Carson and Lirikai.

"I'm sure we'll be exchanging the favor again." Lirikai smiled.

"I look forward to it." Pia said.

"Before we go...Renni, you're still good to send my buddy Ian a signed jersey, right?"

Renni grinned, "Of course. Just text me his address and I'll get it sent out to him."

"Awesome! Scots do love their soccer." Carson grinned.

"I think they call it football," Lirikai said, leaning into Carson. "Let's go so they can ride off together. I want to see more of the city before we leave."

Pia and Renni waved as the couple disappeared around the corner.

Tilting her head back, Pia looked up at the stars, barely visible through the city haze. Renni's fingers slid between hers, pulling her attention.

"Do you want to drive?" he nodded toward his bike.

Normally she would have jumped at the chance. It felt like an eon since she'd last ridden her own motorcycle. Shaking her head and stepping closer to him, she said, "Nah, I want to be able to put my hands on you. Besides, I had a non-club soda drink."

She earned herself a seductive grin that made her breath catch. Her heart tripped at the sudden intensity of his gaze.

"Do you know how amazing you are?"

His voice caressed her. She shivered despite the humid night.

"Sometimes." Her lips curled with mischief. "I think our little cabin is the perfect place for us to admire the stars. It's nice and quiet so you can tell me just how amazing I am, as much as you want."

Renni scoffed. "The crickets and frogs are anything but quiet up there, Pia. They're deafening."

"Not when I'm prowling around."

"I'd rather have you prowling my bed."

She arched a brow. "Would you now?"

He nodded. "Come to think of it, I never did get to rip that dress off of you." His hand slid around her waist, drawing her closer.

Every time he touched her it sent a thrill through her.

Mate.

I know.

"If you insist," she said.

"I do. But I'm also not in a hurry. I intend to rip many things off of you, for a good long time, Pia. Now that I've found you, I don't think I can let you go."

Emotion punched through her at his words.

"I know we said there wouldn't be expectations when we started. No strings. Is that what you still want? Because I want more. So much more. You also have to know, I don't know where my career is going after all this mess; I may have to become a mountain dwelling hermit."

She smiled, sliding her fingers up along his face. "I want all the strings we can find, until we're a tight ball; impossible to untangle."

He laughed.

"What? Big cats like to play, too." She slid her lips over his, teasing him with the tip of her tongue.

"Noble heart, brave deed, steed of steel, and hot as hell."

"I will forever serve as your consort, *my queen*." Renni's grin widened.

"This queen wants her king. Her *Mate*." She stood on tiptoe, ghosting her lips over his. "You were right, I'll always want more."

His erection pressed into her belly.

She slid her hands around his torso and down to squeeze his sculpted ass. Goddess, he had a beautiful ass. "Let's go," she whispered, linking her fingers through his, pulling him toward his *Victory Gunner*, "Don't get caught speeding."

EPILOGUE

A YEAR LATER.

Renni stood on the sidelines of the brand-new pitch, arms crossed as he watched the players stretching before training.

His chest expanded to near painful proportions as he admired the new facility.

Never would he have believed he could be so happy. Truly happy.

He frowned the moment suddenly marred.

"Hey! No hair pulling!" He strode forward before the incident escalated. "There is no hair pulling in soccer."

The player spun on his heels, expression full of feigned contrition. No, more like mischievous guilt. Embarrassment flushed his cheeks as he shot a glance at his victim.

Renni frowned down at the player.

"She started it," he said through gritted teeth.

Renni's glare swung to Ella, who stared at him with wide—too wide—eyes. "What? I didn't do anything."

The grin threatened to crack his resolve. He opened his mouth to speak.

Pia beat him to it. "I think 10 push ups each should even things out."

Both kids groaned. "Come on, coach Jensen, that isn't fair!"

"Start with a jog around the field," Renni said, "Off you go."

The two players drooped with spaghetti arms, feet stomping and scraping the grass, glaring at the coaches then at each other, then back at the coaches again. Pia waved a hand at them, indicating they should get started. "Hurry before you miss Coach Diaz' instruction for this session."

As soon as their backs were turned, Renni let out the laugh he'd been holding back.

"He likes her," he said.

"She likes him." she said.

"Kids." Renni's eyes dropped to Pia's rounded belly.

"Yup. Get used to it," she said, leaning forward to kiss him.

"Glad to see you back early. What do you think of the place?"

He studied her expression as she surveyed the training facility they had worked hard to have built for the kids—kids from all over the region and from all backgrounds—to come and learn the sport.

"It's fantastic seeing it finally finished. I have no doubt these guys will be fancy footing it all over the professional field next door in about a decade. I'm proud of you."

Renni's heart nearly exploded with the unguarded love and pride shining in Pia's eyes as she turned her attention back to his face.

"I really thought my career was done after the robbery and kidnapping. I never would have guessed how those events could have brought the community so much closer together. The cooperation between the department and the club...so quick to respond to Ella's kidnapping, really opened the eyes of the people to see just what we can do when we work together."

She laughed, "And how quick they were to throw their money at the project was just phenomenal. And the funding for the under-privileged kids, too."

"Definitely got this place built fast. No complaints here." He studied her face. "Having it up and running early gives us more time for the coming weeks." His palm slid over her belly. His hand bounced when a hard kick hit his palm. "Did you feel that?" he gasped.

Pia laughed, "How could I not? Your budding soccer star has been kicking my insides for weeks now."

He nodded. "Good. Strong legs. I can work with that."

"Are you ready?"

Looking from her belly to her eyes again, he nodded. "Absolutely. Are you?"

"I have no choice. Cole and Maeda refuse to give me anymore assignments for awhile. I have nothing left to do but make sure I can still fit into the wedding dress next week and learn how to change diapers before the time comes."

"Your squad is coming to the wedding?"

Pia nodded, "I'm so excited to see everyone again. *Everyone* is coming! I can't believe so many people RSVP'd."

"You're going to wear your diamond necklace?"

She nodded. "Of course. You're going to rip the dress off me after the wedding?"

"You want me to rip your wedding dress?" He couldn't stop his mouth from gaping.

"Absolutely. I don't intend to ever wear it again." She grinned.

"Fair enough." He pulled her close so he could taste her lips.

A moment later her hands gripped his ass.

"Pia, there are kids around." he said, looking over her shoulder toward the players going through their warmup in the middle of the field.

"They're not looking," she said against his lips.

Two voices giggled from behind him.

Pia's face turned pink, releasing him instantly. "I forgot about those two," she whispered, wide-eyed.

"Don't worry, I always figure out what to tell their parents, when they call."

He continued to hold her pressed to him. The kicks continued from her belly against his. He looked down between them in time to see the top of her belly lurch to one side then settle.

"Does that hurt?"

She shook her head.

"Well, you know we'll need ten more of those to have a complete team to dominate the world with."

She threw her head back and laughed. "We can have fun trying."

Renni smiled at her enthusiasm. "I love you, Pia."

Her eyes glistened up at him, her expression changing from mirth to adoration. "You are my *mate*, Renni. I'll love you forever," she said before pressing her lips to his.

Yes, this—this right here, was Renni's heaven.

~

Read bonus chapter ***The Mating***
https://bit.ly/3GIFL4f

~

Carson & Lirikai   Ian & Raya   Magnus & Ana   Renni & Pia

The Global Paranormal Security Agency

Thank You!

Dear Reader,

Thank you so much for taking the time to read *Prowler*. If you enjoyed it, please consider leaving a review on your favourite platform.

I have more GPSA *Cuffs & Claws* books coming soon featuring the other members of Pia's squad.

For free downloads, to join my newsletter and browse my growing library for more books with *Romance, Adventure and Passion*, visit

JodiKendrick.com

-Jodi

Dragon Island

Dragon Heat

Enchanted Ardor

Wish

EveL Worlds : FUCN'A

Tough Nut
Diamond in the Ruff
Honeyed Nut
Gorilla in the Hiss
FUCN'A Collection One
Pedigree Collection

Finely Aged

Dragon Steel

Global Paranormal Security Agency

Awakened
Surfacing
Polestar
Aquatic Investigations
Prowler

The Kindred Chronicles

Healer
Mercenary

The Soaring Dragon Chronicles

Return Flight
Changeling

About the Author

Jodi Kendrick lives in Eastern Ontario Canada with her *Favourite Person* and chompy furbaby, while their adult children explore the wider world.

As a romance author, she writes in paranormal, fantasy, steampunk & gaslamp subgenres, and sometimes delves into urban fantasy and paranormal women's fiction. Her characters are often quirky, sometimes cranky, but they all woman-up and get the job done while their partners ensure they survive with all their bits and bobs attached.

A history enthusiast and word dabbler most of her life, she enjoys exploring 'beyond-the-everyday' and the 'time-before-now', discovering relationship threads weaving individuals through time and place. She's rarely seen without flashy notebooks and colourful pens.

Follow Jodi on Social Media:

www.ingramcontent.com/pod-product-compliance
Lightning Source LLC
Chambersburg PA
CBHW020212260626
47156CB00002B/339